PRAISE

If You Lived Here You'd Already Be Home

"You may think you've read enough stories about penniless gay clowns who can't get over the loss of a dog, but—I assure you—you have not. John Jodzio is the best kind of modern fiction writer: a thematic traditionalist who feels totally new."

—Chuck Klosterman, author of *Sex, Drugs, and Cocoa Puffs*

"John Jodzio's wonderful collection, *If You Lived Here You'd Already Be Home*, is a set of colorful and seemingly fractured tales, each shining brilliantly alone, but also growing more vibrant as one story lays over another. Together they form an intricately stained glass window that looks out onto a whole new world."

—Hannah Tinti, author of *The Good Thief*

Get In If You Want to Live

"*Get In If You Want to Live* is lovely and captivating. Every page looks great."

—Fred Armisen, *Saturday Night Live* and *Portlandia*

"John Jodzio is one of those weirdos that is fun to spend time with—not in real life, of course, but on the page—because his stories are laugh-out-loud funny and have a strange, uncanny, and memorable edge to them. And even if you don't like to read, his book has cool pictures. It was totally worth the $200 I paid for it."

—Dan Chaon, author of *Await Your Reply*

"*Get In If You Want to Live* is full of genuine laughs for the LOL generation. It's fantastical whimsy meets potty-mouth, gutter-mind brilliance with some beautifully twisted artwork to accompany poignantly filthy stories."

—Kat George, *Thought Catalog*

KNOCKOUT

STORIES

JOHN JODZIO

SOFT SKULL PRESS
AN IMPRINT OF COUNTERPOINT / BERKELEY

Library of Congress Cataloging-in-Publication Data Is Available

Cover design by Matt Dorfman
Interior design by Elyse Strongin. Neuwirth & Associates

ISBN 978-1-59376-635-1

Soft Skull Press
An Imprint of Counterpoint
2560 Ninth Street, Suite 318
Berkeley, CA 94710
www.softskull.com

Printed in the United States of America
Distributed by Publishers Group West

10987654321

For Kate and Theo

TABLE OF CONTENTS

KNOCKOUT

GREAT ALCOHOLIC-OWNED BED AND BREAKFASTS OF THE EASTERN SEABOARD

Me and the boy are out back shooting holes in the rusted-out johnboat when I hear the wheels of a suitcase bump over the cobble of the front path. It's still light out and I'm halfway through my bottle of Beam, which, if I'm pacing myself correctly, means it's five or six o'clock.

"Hop to it," I tell the boy.

The boy isn't mine. He's my dead wife Sandy's, from her dead ex-husband, Jerold. He's blond haired and fine boned. The house we live in is a weathered Victorian that Sandy and I bought to fix up into a bed and breakfast. I got about as far as painting the sign out front with a couple of intertwined roses and the word "Bed" before Sandy died. There was talk after the funeral that the boy would go to live with some of Jerold's relatives in Ohio, but when it came down to it none of them would actually drive down here to pick him up.

I watch the boy skip off. He's eleven and he runs like he's got a corncob up his ass. I try not to hold that against him. I don't run like that and I do not look like him in the least, but he hasn't ever called me anything other than Dad. I'll tell him about his real father very soon, I suppose. I've thought the conversation all out. I want to do it when I am sober, which usually means right away in the morning. I'm planning on telling him over steak and eggs. I'll sit him down at the kitchen table and tell him I've got something important to say. He's smart, this boy, very inquisitive. I know how the conversation will go. He'll start in with the questions before I've even started saying what needs to be said.

"Is this the sex talk?" he'll ask.

"More or less," I'll say.

I lean the rifle against the woodpile and walk around to the front of the house. There's a woman standing there. She's in her late thirties, wearing a baseball hat and sunglasses. I can't see her eyes, but I can tell by the tilt of her head she's glancing up at the gable, looking at how it's leaning some, not ready to fall or anything, but nowhere near straight. The boy does exactly what I've taught him to do anytime someone shows up on our doorstep—he grabs her luggage and hauls it up the stairs before she can change her mind.

"What brings you here, ma'am?" he asks.

The boy is having trouble lifting her suitcase. He's bouncing it up the stairs, so I grab onto the handle and help him out. I can understand why he's struggling. It's heavy as hell; it must weigh a hundred pounds.

"Are there gold bars in here?" I ask the woman. "Or a dead body?"

The woman gives me a wincing smile. She hardly has any legs under her. She got these stubby things, hardly worth a glance. Sandy, now that was a lady. Long legs and a mouth that could let out a deep and powerful moan.

"I'm writing a travel guide," she says.

I don't know what that has to do with a heavy suitcase, but I don't press her. I've only got two rules to stay here. Number one, you pay what you owe, and number two, don't shoot, stab, or poison me or the boy.

"I'm staying at all of the B and Bs up and down the Eastern Seaboard," she says. She takes another look up at the roof, right near that hole in the soffit where the raccoon lives. "And this is on my list of places to review."

We haven't had a guest in a month, but the boy hasn't forgotten the protocol. He asks for a credit card for room deposit and incidentals. He runs an imprint on our credit card machine. He looks at the name on the card, hands it back.

"Thank you, Ms. Brunell," he says.

The boy is polite and does well in school. When I go to teacher's conferences I can't get his teachers to say anything bad about him. He does his homework, shares, makes friends easily.

"Can I have a room with southern exposure?" Ms. Brunell asks.

I pluck a room key from the board underneath the till.

"Let's put Ms. Brunell in the Grover Cleveland Suite," I say.

The boy likes presidents so we named all of our rooms after the fat ones. While the Grover Cleveland Suite isn't as big as the William Howard Taft Room, it's the quietest. If I would actually get around to trimming the dogwood out back, the room would have a great view of the river. Right now about the only thing you can see is the swing set in the backyard of my neighbor Masoli's house. I really hope Ms. Brunell takes into account all the potential we have here. I hope she can see what we could become, even though we won't.

The boy shows her to her room, and I hear Ms. Brunell drawing a bath, the pipes hissing and clacking.

"What do you think she'll write about us?" the boy asks over the noise.

"Only good things," I yell back.

How Sandy died was a dumbass thing. One night, on her way to meet me at the Keg n' Cork, she tried to go around a railroad barrier. Her car was speared by the front of the train, pushed all the way through our town, sparking and screeching, right past the courthouse and right past the barstool where I sat waiting for her. She went past the Riverwalk Mall and into Halsford before the conductor could get that fucking train stopped. The police report said she died in Halsford, but the coroner's report said that she died on impact, and while it can't really be both, it is.

The boy was a year and a half when that happened. Up until that point, I hadn't done much for him other than read him some bedtime stories and change the occasional diaper, but over the next few years, I did it all. My grief was not helped by the fact that each time I looked at the boy's face I saw Sandy, and each time I thought of Sandy a curl of pain rippled across my chest—a feeling like something had been torn out of me and then that very same thing had been rolled in glass and shoved back in me upside down.

"That'll go away soon," my sister, Marlene, told me.

"If it was going away it would have gone away by now," I told her. "I'm stuck with it."

I stopped drinking after Sandy died, but when the boy started kindergarten, I started up again. I ended up drinking on the job and I got fired when I cut off the tip of my pinky with a band saw. This started a long period of the boy and me making due, of one day melting into the next, of the occasional guest or two stumbling onto our doorstep. By now, the boy and I have developed a solid routine. He knows he can count on me to make him breakfast and hand him a bag lunch on the way to school. When he gets home, he knows that he'll be the one making dinner and helping me up to bed.

The boy chops up some onions for a stew and I go back outside and shoot some more holes in the boat. While I'm out there I see Masoli and his six-year-old daughter, April, smacking a beach ball back and forth in their front yard. When Masoli first moved in we got along great; I lent him my socket set and he lent me his hedge trimmer. One night I invited him over for a barbeque. While our kids played together, we ate ribs and talked about how my wife was dead and how his ex-wife was batshit crazy.

"After I got custody she was so angry she lit my '77 Corvette on fire. I spent ten years restoring that car and she burned it to a crisp in ten minutes."

For a while I imagined Masoli and me becoming good friends, drinking beer, and shooting the shit. I pictured us commiserating about single parenting and keeping each other sane. None of that happened. A few nights after that barbeque, I got blind drunk and walked into Masoli's front yard without any pants on and he punched me in the face. We haven't talked since.

I hear April squeal as Masoli bats the beach ball way over her head. Sometimes when they're outside goofing around, I grab the boy and we stand on our driveway and laugh really loud so Masoli knows we're having fun too. I go inside now and pull the boy onto the porch and we fake laugh loud enough to drown out April's giggling.

"You ready for dinner?" the boy asks when we're finished.

I pump a couple more shots into the hull of the boat, and then I pick up a few of the bigger rocks from my driveway and chuck them over into Masoli's yard so they'll fuck up his lawn mower.

"Now I'm ready," I say.

The next morning I make biscuits and redeye gravy. Sandy and I started dating when we were working together at a diner in New Orleans called the HunGree Bear. She was a waitress and I was the cook. We lit out of there right before Katrina, grabbing everything we could and throwing it in the back of my truck. We got out of there just in time, but we couldn't find our dog, McGruff, before we left. Sometimes at night I dream McGruff's on one of those incredible journeys. In my dream, he always shows up on our porch with a bunch of burrs and sticks matted in his fur, thinner, but not all that worse for wear. I've been thinking about getting another dog for a while now, but for some reason I still think McGruff's coming back. I don't want him to be pissed that I thought he wasn't.

"I trust your night was pleasant," I say to Ms. Brunell as she sits down at the breakfast table.

"Pleasant enough," she says.

She's wearing a track suit. She still has on her sunglasses. I can't tell if she's got a decent body underneath her baggy clothes, but I'm leaning toward no.

"Are you going to look around town today or go hiking by the river?" I ask her while I stir the gravy. This is a good batch, thick enough to not run everywhere, thin enough to get into the nooks and crannies of the biscuit.

"I might lay low," she says. "I'm not feeling the best."

I put a plate of biscuits in front of her and she takes a bite. There's a spot of mold on the wall above her head that I keep painting over but that keeps coming back.

"I wasn't expecting much," Ms. Brunell says, pointing at the biscuits with her fork, "but these are damn good."

I wonder if she should be taking notes for her review, but maybe she's got a better memory than me. I decide to try to be on my best behavior for however long she stays, drink less than usual. Maybe my breakfasts will be the thing that wins her over; maybe my cooking can make up for everything that's fucked up around here.

I get the boy off to school and then I spend the rest of my morning napping under the dogwood. When I wake up, I see Ms. Brunell standing in the window with a pair of binoculars up to her face.

Great, I think, she's into birds. Maybe we can take a stroll along the trail and I can point out where all the reticulated woodpeckers nest. Maybe we'll take a walk through the marsh and I can show her that family of owls that lives inside that hollowed-out sycamore.

When I get back inside, Ms. Brunell is sitting in the living room in front of the fireplace, staring into its blackened mouth. I would love to light a fire for her, but a dead squirrel got stuck in the flue a couple of weeks ago. The smell isn't that bad unless it gets really windy. Just in case she's got a really sensitive nose, I light a scented candle.

"What other bed and breakfasts have you stayed at?" I ask her.

"I've been up and down the coast," she says. "Tons of places."

I mention a couple of other B and Bs around here—the Carriage House, the Mount Angel House, the Geffon-Buckley Bed and Breakfast. These places are clean and quaint, full of flowery wallpaper and potpourri, packed almost every weekend. Those places are how our place was supposed to turn out. I can only imagine what those places say about us if anyone asks. And I doubt anyone asks.

"All of those are on my list," Ms. Brunell says. "I'm going to stay at the Mount Angel House right after this."

"I saw you with your binoculars earlier," I tell her. "There's good birding around here. If you're interested, I could show you some owls later tonight."

I'm trying to go the extra mile for Ms. Brunell so she'll give us a decent review, but I suspect she's used to better offers than dumb-ass owls. The fancier places probably pull out all the stops; give her gift baskets full of fine chocolates and cheeses to help her remember her stay.

"Yes, owls might be nice," she says to me as she lies down on the couch and closes her eyes.

I'm shooting some beer bottles off the back fence with the pump rifle when the boy comes home with his report card. The thing is perfect, straight As. His teachers have filled up the comments sections with great things about his attitude and work ethic. I hand him a twenty from my wallet. I tell him to spend it on something frivolous, like candy or fireworks, like I would've when I was young.

"Sure," he tells me. "Okay."

Even though he says this, I know he won't spend it on anything good. He'll tuck it away in the shoebox he keeps under his bed for household emergencies. If I want him to have fireworks or candy, I'll probably need to buy them myself.

While we're resetting the bottles on the fence, we hear a loud squawking noise near the house. The boy and I run over and see a hawk fighting with the raccoon that lives up in the soffit. A family of hawks nested there before the raccoons and now I suppose one of them has returned to find someone else has invaded their roost. The hawk and the raccoon are really going at it, the hawk flapping and screaming and the raccoon clawing and hissing. I fire my gun in the air to break things up, but it doesn't do anything. I fire again, this time a little closer to them, and my shot scares off the hawk, but I accidentally hit the raccoon in the gut. It scrambles back inside my roof and then it starts to bellow. The boy and I watch as a shitload of raccoon blood starts to pour out of the soffit, a river of red running down the side of the house, right over Ms. Brunell's window.

By the time the boy comes back with the ladder, the raccoon is dead and the house is caked in blood.

"Keep Brunell busy," I tell him. "Don't let her go back to her room until I can get this crap cleaned off her window, okay?"

I grab a bucket and a sponge and climb up the ladder. While I'm scrubbing, I can't help but look inside Ms. Brunell's room. There's a black bra hung on the doorknob. Her bird-watching binoculars are lying on the bed. There's other stuff there too, weird things. Laid out on the desk are a dozen pictures of Masoli's daughter, April, when she was younger. There are also a few pictures of Ms. Brunell, Masoli, and April on the desk—one of them standing in front of the Grand Canyon. In another, the three of them are standing on the deck of a cruise ship with the endless blue of the ocean behind them. Ms. Brunell's suitcase is open on the floor next to her bed and I can see now why it was so heavy—it's filled with a couple of handguns, a tent, some cans of food. It's taken me a minute to connect the dots—that Ms. Brunell is actually April's mom, that she's Masoli's ex-wife, that she's here to steal April—but when I do, I quit cleaning the blood off the window and scramble down the ladder to tell Masoli.

Before I can get over to Masoli, he starts up his lawn mower. And while I'm running toward him I hear a loud crunch, one of the rocks I've tossed into his yard hitting the blade. There's a puff of blue smoke and his mower grinds to a halt. Masoli flips it over, sees a huge gouge in the blade and a rock that matches the rock from my driveway. When he looks up, he sees me coming toward him—drunk and out of breath, raccoon blood smeared down the front of my shirt. April is jumping rope in his driveway. When she sees me, she stops.

"Turn your ass around," Masoli tells me.

I keep walking toward him. He tells April to go inside and then he marches toward me, his hands already clenched into fists.

"Get out of my yard now," Masoli says.

"Hold on, hold on," I say. "I need to tell you something."

I hold my palms up to show him I mean no harm, but Masoli doesn't care. He shoots his right fist through my palms and hits me in the mouth. I feel my teeth dig into my tongue and the bones in my jaw slide upward and I taste blood. I grab my face and topple to the ground in a lump.

As Masoli is walking away from me, the boy flies out of our front door. He screams as he leaps on Masoli's back, flails at Masoli's chest with his spindly arms. The boy gets in a couple of good shots before Masoli tosses him off and stomps back inside his house.

"That motherfucker is going to get his," I tell the boy as we lie there in the grass. "Don't you worry about that."

"Okay," the boy says. "Sure."

There's conviction in my voice, but not in the boy's. I can tell he's tired of defending me. I want to explain to him how this time was different, how my intentions were pure, how what happened was unprovoked. I want to tell him I was trying to help but things went sideways. I keep my mouth shut because I can tell that no matter what I say, he's already grouped this together with all the other dumb things I've done.

After the boy is in bed, I lie down on the couch in the living room. Around midnight Ms. Brunell comes downstairs. It's windy outside; it's getting ready to storm. The room is dark; she doesn't notice I'm lying there. I could say something, try to intervene, but I don't. I let whatever's going to happen, happen.

After she walks out the door, I twist off the top of a bottle of Beam and pour out a couple of fingers into a lowball. I stand on my front porch as the rain grows harder, the wind stripping the leaves from the trees. At some point I know I'm going to need to go down to the basement and spread out bath towels where the foundation leaks. After that I'll need to set a bucket in the upstairs bathroom to collect all the water that drips from the ceiling. Ms. Brunell is dressed in all black, black hoodie, black stocking cap. She pries open Masoli's basement window with a crowbar and slips inside his house. When she slides out the front door a few minutes later, April is asleep in her arms. I watch her drive away and then I take a piece of scrap paper and write the boy a note that says "Steak and Eggs for Breakfast." I write it in big, dark letters and I leave it on his bedside table so he'll be sure to see it right away when he wakes up.

KNOCKOUT

When I was in rehab, my roommate Tommy showed me how to knock out animals by pinching a spot on the back of their necks. I mostly practiced on the rehab cat but I also practiced on the overnight counselor, Jeff, who sort of looked like a cat. Sometimes I would sneak up behind Jeff and touch him on the neck and he'd zonk out. The rehab place was near a zoo and after we'd knock out Jeff, Tommy and I would steal the keys to his Corolla and drive over there. One time we found a ladder and knocked out a giraffe. That was probably my favorite time at the zoo. The giraffe was very elegant in the way it fell, slowly dropping to its knees and then gently tipping over on its side with a slight puff of breath.

After I finished my stint at rehab, I moved back home with my father. He'd been an insurance salesman, but he'd recently retired. Now, for a hobby, he taught archery to poor kids. Last summer, when I'd been on drugs, he shot me in the thigh with an arrow. I remember that he was trying to teach me some lesson about life. It must not have been very profound, because I could not remember what it was. All I remembered now was the sound of that arrow entering my thigh. It went fffffffftttt. Maybe that was the only lesson that he was trying to teach me. That an arrow entering into your thigh goes fffffffftttt.

I still hung out with Tommy a few nights a week. My father would not allow him inside our house though. He said Tommy reminded him of the all the bad stuff that I'd ever done. Like that time I totaled his Buick as I drove to the pawnshop to sell his coin collection. Or that time I accidentally pitchforked that duck that sometimes waddled into our backyard looking for bread crusts.

"Tommy and I are keeping each other clean," I explained. "In rehab, everyone had fake spiders crawling on them, but Tommy and I had fake ants crawling all over us. We bonded over that shit."

"He'll let you down," my dad said, loading a bunch of arrows into a quiver to take down to the community center. "Or you'll let him down. Letting people down is the only thing you two really have in common."

Even after a couple months of staying sober, my father wouldn't accept Tommy as my friend. One night when Tommy picked me up, my dad ran outside and shot an arrow in the driver-side door of his truck. I apologized to Tommy, but he waved me off.

"People have shot arrows at me before," Tommy said, "and they probably will again."

Lately Tommy and I hung out down by the river. We'd gotten tired of going to the zoo long ago, and the time we'd tried to pick up women at the local pet store by knocking out those chinchillas had been an absolute disaster. Instead of going to AA meetings, we wrestled on the banks of the river to see which one of us could knock the other one out. Once when I knocked Tommy out I pulled down his pants and wrote the word "Jackass" across his ass cheeks in black marker, and the next time he knocked me out he wrote the word "Dummy" on mine. This continued on for the next couple of months, back and forth, sometimes one of us drawing a very funny and detailed picture on the other's butt cheeks or writing a few sentences about our state of mind. Each time I got knocked out I went home and pulled down my pants and pondered Tommy's writings or his cartoons in my bathroom mirror and I thought about how hilarious this whole situation was and how good it was to finally find someone who liked the same things I did. It was great to finally be able to communicate some of my struggles with another human being and also have something interesting they thought be written on my body a few days later. Tommy's writings and cartoons were often very poignant and thoughtful. I really wished my father could see this side of him.

"We're not going to wrestle tonight," Tommy said one night when he picked me up. "We've got a job to do."

"What job?" I asked.

Tommy usually drove with his knees so he could gesture with his hands while he talked. Now he turned toward me and slapped me on the shoulder. At first I thought he was trying to knock me out, but this was just a regular, friendly shoulder slap.

"We're going to steal a tiger and then sell him to this guy I know," he told me.

Tommy turned down a driveway and I saw a small house behind a thin stand of trees. He shut off his headlights but kept the car creeping up the driveway.

"This is it," Tommy said. "The guy keeps a tiger in a cage in his backyard, but he doesn't feed it enough. It's a totally bad situation."

I tried to get a better look inside the house, to see if it looked like there was anyone at home. There were no lights on, but I knew that didn't mean a damn thing. Most tiger owners I knew liked to sit at their kitchen tables and clean their guns and knives by the light of the moon, and I could only assume this tiger owner was exactly the same, sitting in the dark and waiting for that time when he could use those super-clean guns and knives on anyone who tried to steal his pet.

"After we knock it out we're going to throw it in the back of the truck," Tommy told me. "And then we'll drive over to Randy's. He's going to keep the tiger in his basement to scare the shit out of people."

Tommy grabbed the bolt cutter and I followed. I was scared, but mostly what I was thinking about was how we'd get paid some good cash for this and how it would be great to slap a stack of bills down in front of my father and how that stack of bills might prompt my father to finally say he was proud of me.

We walked over to the cage and Tommy was right, the tiger didn't look good. The fur on its chest was rubbed raw and one of its eyes was glassed over with a cataract. His breath kept catching in its throat. The tiger brought its head up to the bars of the cage and I scratched him behind his ears.

"Quit dicking around," Tommy said. "Do it already."

I reached in the cage and pinched the back of the tiger's neck and he slumped over. Tommy opened the lock and we hauled the tiger to the truck.

"When we meet Randy, you need to be cool, okay?" Tommy told me as we drove. "Don't be your normal dumbass self."

I hadn't planned to say a word when we got to Randy's house, because who hadn't heard a story about a stolen tiger deal going sour and someone getting shot up? In my neighborhood you heard these kinds of stories all the time. I knew to keep my mouth shut.

We pulled into the driveway and Randy came running out of his house. It was pretty cold outside to be shirtless and barefoot, but it didn't look like it was bothering Randy all that much.

"Where's my guy?" he yelled to Tommy. "Where's my guy?'

The tiger was still out cold, his tongue lolling around. I could see where muscles had formerly filled his body, where his fur lay slack.

Randy ran his hand over the bare spots on the tiger's fur, then he slid his fingers up the tiger's neck. He shifted his fingers around a couple of times. Then he did it again. He shook his head.

"This tiger you brought me doesn't have a goddamn pulse," he said.

Tommy put his fingers on the tiger's neck, shifted them around.

"It was alive when we stole it," he said. "It must have died on the way here."

"You brought me a dead tiger," Randy said as he walked back toward his house. "When you bring me a live tiger, you get your meth."

Tommy hadn't said anything to me about us stealing the tiger in trade for drugs. I wondered if maybe Randy was mistaken, that maybe Randy had misunderstood Tommy when they'd struck their deal.

"Don't worry," Tommy told me. "I'll get this straightened out."

Tommy followed Randy inside. While I waited, I looked at the tiger. I felt bad about what we'd put it through, what everyone had put it through, that its last moments of life were bumping around in the back of a pickup instead of chasing down a water buffalo on the savannah. A minute or two later, Tommy walked out of the house, smiling.

"I don't know about you," he said, holding up a dime bag, "but I'm sick of everything being stupid and boring."

Tommy shook some of the meth onto his knuckle and snorted. He held out the baggie to me. I also hated how boring and stupid our lives were now. More than that though, I hated how sometimes life threw you a curveball—how you thought you were going to make some money selling a stolen tiger to make your dad proud, but then all the sudden there were drugs instead of money and then you were probably going to relapse mostly because you didn't want to disappoint your best friend who had recently drawn a very funny cartoon about an octopus on your ass cheeks that would not come off your body no matter how hard you scrubbed.

"Before we go on this bender," I told Tommy, "before this all happens, we need to bury the tiger."

"No problem," he said.

We drove back to my house and I snuck inside the garage and grabbed two shovels. Once when I was high I'd stolen my father's old riding lawn mower. I pushed it out of the garage and started it up when I was a block away so he didn't wake up. I drove the mower down the street, right up to the door of the pawnshop and sold it for eighty bucks. My father had bought another lawn mower recently and I ran my hand over it as I walked by, thinking how the new one was probably worth way more.

Tommy and I had decided to bury the tiger by the river. We'd dig a hole and then maybe one of us would say some kind words. After that, after our shoulders ached from digging, we'd get high and drive to the bars downtown. We'd planned all this out already, but when I got back to the truck, I saw Tommy hoovering a line off the hood. The bag was already half gone.

Tommy threw his hair out of his eyes and looked at me. "You're judging me, aren't you? I can feel your judgey-ass eyes all over me."

"I'm not judging you," I said. "I just want to get this tiger in the ground before you get too paranoid to dig."

"You're not going to even get high," Tommy said, pressing his index finger into my chest. "You'll puss out. When it comes to it, you'll start rubbing on your six-month coin and then you'll run to a goddamn meeting and everyone there will say you saved yourself when you ran away from me."

I slapped Tommy's finger away from my chest, but he grabbed onto my forearm. I twisted it away, but then Tommy dropped down and hooked my leg. As we wrestled, I tried to slide my arm around to the back of Tommy's neck to knock him out, but he smacked my hand away. He shoved me down on the front lawn and tried to jump on top of me, but I stuck my foot out and kicked him square in the gut. Tommy reeled back against the truck and stood there for a second catching his breath. As he stood there, a large paw rose up from the payload and slashed across his jacket. Tommy fell forward and I watched as the tiger leapt from the truck and onto Tommy's back. Tommy started screaming and I ran toward him and smacked the tiger in the ribs with the shovel. The tiger was stunned for a second and he rolled off Tommy. But then he charged at me. I dropped the shovel and ran, but he snagged my pant leg with his paws. I kicked at his face, but then he got a hold of my other leg. The tiger began to reel me toward his mouth.

"Knock him out!" I yelled to Tommy, "Knock him out!" But Tommy was gone, running down the block, not looking back.

The tiger pulled me closer, clawing its way up my body. I thought I was done for, but then the motion lights on my front porch kicked on and the entire yard lit up and then there was my father striding toward me, holding up his compound bow, and then ffffffftttt, one into the tiger's chest, and then ffffffftttt, one splitting the tiger's forehead, and then ffffffffttttt, one last arrow into my thigh, deep, deep inside there, so I would never forget.

SOMEDAY ALL OF THIS WILL PROBABLY BE YOURS

My boyfriend, Atomic, is speed dating.

A bell rings, he moves on to another woman.

It's a Mexican restaurant and I'm stuck outside. I press my face against the window and see Atomic sitting in a high-backed chair across from a blonde woman sipping a margarita. He's already beautiful, but we took twenty-five bucks and got him a haircut, just in case. We went over to Men's Wearhouse and shoplifted a shirt and a tie. He took out his nose ring and slid it into my ear.

"It's an investment," he told me before he walked inside. "This night is an investment in us."

The bell rings again and Atomic slides over to another table, gives a big smile to a mousy-looking brunette.

"Should I call myself William?" he asked me. "Or is Willem sexier?"

I stand out in the cold. My name is still my name. I still look how I look. I still love Atomic the most of anyone I've ever loved.

"Wait right here," Atomic said. "This won't take long."

I try to wait, but like always I'm no good at it. I rewrap my coat around my body and then do it again because it doesn't feel right. I button and rebutton the buttons, but that doesn't work. My coat feels crooked and even though it is freezing out, I take it off and put it back on, over and over, until it feels exactly right.

I wipe the fog of my breath away from the window. I try to figure out which lonely woman Atomic will go home with, which woman he is going to tie up and not untie until she gives him her PIN number.

"If you don't fuck everything up," Atomic told me before he went inside, "this plan will work great."

Another bell rings. Atomic grins at a woman with horse teeth. A bus passes and shields me from the wind for a few seconds. A show has just let out at the movie theatre down the block and I watch everyone sprint to their cars. I lean into the building, hope for a little heat to leak out of the bricks.

Sometimes at parties or at the bar, people ask Atomic and I how we met.

"We were high school sweethearts," he'll lie.

"We worked at a mystery dinner theatre together," he'll say.

"She saved me from drowning," he'll tell them.

Atomic's a good liar. He's funny, he's charming. He has kissable lips, good teeth. He knows that everyone would rather hear something interesting than something true.

Here's how we actually met: A year ago I got pissed off at my last boyfriend and I got on a Greyhound bus. When I got off, Atomic was standing in front of a building hitting a pickle bucket with some drumsticks.

He said, "Hey you, come here," to me.

And that's what I did.

I can't wait any longer, so I don't. I walk inside the bar and find a table with some nametags on it. I take one that says "Ms. Rita Johnstone" and peel off the backing. I slap it on my shirt above my tit.

The bell rings again and instead of looking around like I'm lost, I sit down across the table from a man with a nametag that says "Stephen." He's wearing a navy-blue sweater. His skin has a grayish tint, the color of canned meat.

"I'm Rita," I say. "Sorry I'm late."

I read somewhere that if you say something over and over again enough times to yourself you will begin to believe it. Other people have told me this is true, that if you repeat something enough your brain will finally just give up and make whatever you keep repeating your new reality.

"Yep," I tell Stephen. "I'm Rita, Rita, Rita."

Even though it is the middle of winter, Stephen's sweating. Beads of sweat form under his wispy hair and he wipes them off with his sleeve. The sweat immediately forms again. This time he takes a paper napkin and dabs it away. Unfortunately the napkin is maroon and it leaves a burgundy stain on his forehead.

"I work in the restaurant supply business," he tells me. "I can get you stuff at cost."

"Wow," I say. "What stuff?"

I've decided to say everything in this little girl voice, high and squeaky. I notice there are little pockets of spit forming in the corners of Stephen's mouth.

"Industrial mixers, pots and pans," he says. "Professional ovens, pastry racks, ramekins."

"That's incredible," I tell him.

"What do you do?" he asks.

I tell him I'm a pediatric nurse, even though I really work part-time at a sandwich shop. I make up a sick child for my lie too, a boy named Eric who has bad lungs. I tell Stephen all about Eric, how each breath he takes is a struggle, how inspirational he is to everyone in the ward. I tell him how Eric drew a picture of me with angel wings and how I framed it and hung it right above my bed so that each morning I'll see it and remember how precious life really is.

"You sound like a saint," Stephen says.

"Part saint," I say, "and part sinner." I wink at Stephen as I say the word "sinner" and he nearly chokes on his drink.

The bell rings again and Atomic sits down next to a woman with a dark-brown bob who has a ring on each of her fingers. I flop down in front of a man named Graham. Graham is skinny and bald, with a crooked nose. He tells me he works as an urban planner. He says he has a condo with a view of the river. He takes a cloth from his pocket and wipes off his glasses and I take a tortilla chip from the basket in front of me and put it in my mouth and crunch down.

"Do you like my mouth?" I ask him. "Some people have told me they really like my mouth. Some people say that it's the best part of me."

"It's a good mouth," Graham says.

Someone has left a cocktail napkin with some questions on it at our table and I start asking Graham these questions rapid fire, not leaving him any chance to answer.

Where do you see yourself in five years, how do you feel about kids, if I went blind or lost my legs would you stick by me, what is your spirit animal, what's a perfect day to you, how long is a long backrub, do you have any hang-ups about psoriasis?

Other than the psoriasis question, these are the kinds of things I often ask Atomic. He gets annoyed at me when I do this, calls me "Magazine Quiz." Jesus, he'll say, we might not be alive in five minutes and here you are wasting your time with this?

When I run out of questions on the napkin, I start making up some questions of my own.

"How do you want to die?" I ask Graham.

"Fire," he says immediately. He seems like he has actually prepared for this question, which I appreciate.

"Really?" I say. "Me too."

"It would hurt for a bit," he says, "but then it wouldn't really matter, right?"

After I'm done with the questions, Graham goes into his bag and pulls out a cardboard tube and spreads some onion skin sheets out over our table.

"This is my latest project," he explains. "Here's the green space, here's the ample parking. The bottom floor is zoned for mixed use."

I can tell he's testing me, seeing if I like the same things that excite him. So I show him that they do. I run my fingers along the edges of the blue-lined paper. I ask him questions about his project, I smile and nod at his answers.

"Things get torn down," he tells me just before the bell rings again, "and then new things push out of the earth to fill the void. It's like a new tooth cutting through your gums to replace what's missing."

I sit down across from Atomic. His nametag says "Willem." It has started to peel off his chest, but he presses it back down, smooths it out.

"Jesus Christ," he whispers, "I told you to wait outside."

"I got bored," I say.

"You always get bored," he says. "What if I got bored with how bored you get? What would happen then?"

A few months ago Atomic tied me to a chair. He said it was an experiment to help me learn more about myself. When he left to go get some cigarettes, I chewed through the twine he tied me up with, something he hadn't figured I'd be able to do. The next time he was more careful. He handcuffed me to the door of our refrigerator.

"You're going to ruin it," he says. "You're going to fuck up the plan."

I look around at the other people here, lonely people trying to put their best foot forward, people who weren't ready to meet someone when they still looked good enough, people who work too many hours, people who drink too much or can't stop themselves from doing weird shit, like going to grocery stores and breaking all the candy bars in half when no one is looking.

"Let's go live in the country," I tell Atomic. "We'll open a restaurant. You'll flip the burgers and I'll bring out the plates. We'll grow some weed in the basement of our house and sell it to all the high school kids. We'll have a kid and name it Atomic Jr. and call it Tommy for short."

He shakes his head no.

"This is going to work," he says. "It'll work if you'd just have a little patience."

The bell rings twice in a row and the speed dating ends. We fill out an index card to say who we liked best. I give Willem the highest rating, even though I know he doesn't exist. Graham is my second choice because at least he and I know how we want to die. I watch as everyone gathers up their coats. Some of them look giddy, but there are other ones, ones who haven't made a match, who slink away. Atomic makes his way over to the bar with the blonde woman with the horse teeth. I sit across the bar from him now, wrapping and unwrapping my coat.

Don't, I think, don't. I try to make this word enter the blonde woman's brain—get her to stop. It's not working though, my telepathy; the blonde woman keeps twirling her hair, gulping her margarita. My powers of suggestion are weak and the waiters, dressed in those stupid Cuban shirts, keep cutting through my view, running baskets of chips, huge drinks, sizzling and steaming platters of food, their trays held up to the heavens like they are offering up a sacrifice to some enchilada-loving god.

"You'll follow me back," Atomic told me, "and after I tie her up, I'll let you in."

Don't, I keep thinking, but this woman isn't listening. She's happy to be talking to Atomic, so beautiful and so interested in her. She's drunk and she's telling herself this is real. She's probably telling that to herself over and over because that's what she wants to believe.

I run to the bathroom and while I'm there, I think about ruining the plan. I think about walking up to Atomic and saying something like, "I've been looking all over for you. Your mother just had a stroke." Or maybe I'll just yell at him like I'm a jilted lover.

When I get back out to the bar there are now two women sitting next to Atomic, the woman with the horse teeth and a new woman with short black hair and glasses. I wonder where she came from, but I don't have long to mull it over, because all three of them stand up, put on their coats, and leave.

They walk out the door and down the street, arm in arm in arm. They skip for half a block. What the hell is he doing? Is he going to tie both of them up, bleed both of their bank accounts dry?

The three of them walk past that coffee shop where I worked for a week before I got fired. They duck into a loading dock. I stand across the street and watch Atomic kiss the blonde woman. After he is finished kissing her, he kisses the brunette. Then the two women kiss. They pull apart and giggle for a second, but Atomic takes the back of their heads and pushes them back together.

"Whatever you see isn't real," Atomic told me before he went into the restaurant, "whatever you see is just acting, okay?"

They stumble down the block. Soon both of the women guide Atomic up the steps of a condo. I see the lights turn on inside. I crouch right underneath the window. There are no cars around and I hear the clinking of glassware inside. It's snowing now, huge flakes.

I wait for Atomic to tie them up and let me in, but there's nothing. I wait ten minutes, twenty minutes, still nothing. While I'm standing there, a car pulls up across the street and honks at me. And then it honks again. I hear someone call out for Rita.

"Rita?" he says again. I do not answer him because that's not my name. I do not answer him because I'm hiding in some bushes outside a stranger's condo.

"Rita?" he yells out. "Everything okay?"

I climb out of the shrubbery and see Graham sitting in his idling car.

"I saw you run out of the bar," he says. "I'm not normally this creepy. I just wanted to make sure you got home okay."

I try to look inside the condo, but the blinds are closed. All I can see is the flicker of candlelight; all I can hear now are murmurings, maybe some light moaning. I know that I need to go now, that waiting here any longer will be horrible for me.

"Hold on," I tell Graham.

I grab a piece of landscape brick from a retaining wall in front of the condo and I rear back and throw it through the window. I watch as the glass explodes and then I hear the screams from inside. I sprint to Graham's car.

"Drive," I tell him.

A few blocks later, I realize I'm still wearing my nametag, "Ms. Rita Johnstone," and I rip it off me. I crumple it up and throw it out the window.

"My real name's Ellen," I tell Graham.

Graham turns left, heads back toward downtown.

"Nice to meet you, Ellen," he says. "Where do you want me to take you?"

"Show me something," I say.

We drive for a few minutes and then Graham pulls up next to a construction site. It's about half done, mostly just girders, the outline of what it will be.

"This is what I'm working on now. It's an up-and-coming neighborhood," he tells me. "There's a coffee shop going up over there. There's going to be a new grocery store around the corner."

Graham gets out of the car and I follow him. We stare through the chain link fence into the construction site. Graham keeps talking and pointing. I'm cold, so I lean into him and he puts his arm around me. The snow has placed a soft cover over everything hard and I close my eyes and turn toward his face and wait patiently for him to press his lips against my lips.

THE WEDDING PARTY

Cantwell found the dead horse near the dry creek. There was a neon-green Post-it note slapped on the horse's flank with the word "Sorry" written on it. The word was scribbled in blue glitter pen and the "o" in "sorry" was shaped like a goddamn heart.

The early morning sky was orange but would not be for much longer. Cantwell's bad hip said rain, but his trick knee said no way. He leaned against the hood of his truck and pulled out his cell phone and dialed up Lupe. While he waited for him to answer, Cantwell's eyes scanned back across the pasture. The destruction started at the county road. Muddy tire ruts that dropped down from the tar. A gaping hole in the west-edge fence. Shitty after shitty spirographed in the pasture grass. The horse lay at the end of a long skid, its ribs bayonetted through its midriff. Around its torso was a pool of blood that hadn't yet settled into the loam. Cantwell fished the bottle of whiskey he'd dug out of the snake-bite kit and took a long pull.

"Hello?" Lupe said.

"When you come in," Cantwell told him, "bring your digging gloves."

Last summer, the owner of the Tanglewood Ranch, Tee Dennison, had transformed the ranch into a wedding venue. With this change, he turned Cantwell into a cowboy who barely cowboyed. Instead of mending fences, Cantwell drove a pickup to the discount liquor store in Kalispell. Instead of loading hay bales, he filled his payload with vodka and beer.

Cantwell had nearly quit ten times since. Every time he voiced his displeasure, Dennison went into his safe and pulled out a thick stack of twenties. He pushed them across his desk to Cantwell and told him he was sorry but that this was the way it was now. Dennison knew full well that Cantwell had a daughter in college and that he still paid the tab for his ex-wife's twice-a-week dialysis. Cantwell had a weakness for tax-free cash and he always shoved the money into his pocket.

It wasn't just the new job that burned Cantwell's ass lately. The town of Junction Creek was creeping closer to the ranch. The county had started to parcel out acreage last summer. They divided and subdivided, curbed and guttered. Five years ago, the ranch was the only place for twenty square miles. Cantwell remembered sitting in the field on summer nights, shit-faced, tracing constellations with his index finger, one dot to the next. Developers had ruined all of that. They snaked winding sidewalks up to oak doors. They shoved streets signs into the dirt. They put up halogen streetlights that made the stars look hazy and small.

Cantwell was overjoyed when the housing market went tits up. The developers sent their crews home and now all that remained on the hills above the ranch were house frames. At dusk they looked to him like the old ribs of beached whales, picked over and bleached by the sun.

"Already got something in your bonnet?" the chef, Jen Purvey, asked as Cantwell trudged back to the truck. He had a bag of quick lime draped over his shoulder and he was short of breath.

Purvey reached into a plastic storage bin and scattered a handful of croutons for the pond ducks. The birds were already the size of small turkeys. They were so fat that Cantwell suspected that come October there would be no way they'd be able to gain lift-off.

"Those birds know about that set of fancy German knives you got inside?" he asked. "They know that their next stop is a stew?"

Purvey handfulled another mound of croutons out onto the crushed rock of the paddock. She was middle-aged and wide-hipped. While Cantwell didn't like all the turns the ranch had taken recently, she wasn't bad. Each night there was a plate of grub in the walk-in for him to take up and microwave in his room. Every morning there was a thermos of coffee and a blueberry muffin sitting on a silver tray in the foyer.

"Me and the birds have come to an understanding," she told him. "They've traded their lives for these easy weeks of day-old sourdough."

Purvey walked back into the kitchen and Cantwell went into the barn to get a pickaxe. Still calling it a barn was a misnomer—last year it had been expanded and the stables had been remodeled into a reception hall. The hall was retrofitted with a projection screen and surround sound and a parquet floor for dancing. He and Lupe had built the mounts for the speakers and dry-walled the AV booth. They hoisted and electrified the huge chandelier Dennison had found at the architectural salvage place over in Cut Bank.

"Change or adapt," Dennison told Cantwell when he saw his new chandelier hanging down from the rafters. "We change up or our dicks shrivel and die, right?"

"Speak for yourself," he told Dennison.

Cantwell slid the truck through the clumpy fescue back to the dead horse. In his twelve years at the Tanglewood, he had seen a lot of dead shit. Moose and deer and coyotes and foxes. Jackrabbits too numerous to count. Vultures circling dead vultures. Seeing all this dead shit in no way meant he wasn't squeamish about dead shit. Cantwell still hated how dead shit's eyes held a glint of life and how sometimes that glint tricked you into staring deeper—into an abyss so deep and so black thick that it stabbed a reminder into your own chest that your own ticker was only half an inch away from irreparable harm.

He'd lost some weight since his heart attack two summers ago. He'd had to cut new notches in his belt. He still hadn't bought any new pants and the ones he had puckered around his waist.

He parked the truck and hoisted himself out of the cab. As he walked toward the horse, he caught his shadow in the dirt—his legs looking like a bowed clothespin. If he did not hurry, the flies would catch the scent and descend upon the animal. Cantwell spit his chaw into the scrub and shoved his spade into the dirt.

There was another wedding happening that night. From where he dug, Cantwell could see two women connecting the aluminum tines for the balloon arch. Earlier that morning, before he'd driven the fences, a man had driven over from Grey Eagle and dropped off the caged doves. Cantwell was responsible for their release during the ceremony.

"All you need to do," the guy told Cantwell, loud and halting, like Cantwell was deaf, "is open the door. The birds. Will know. What to do. After that."

When Lupe drove up, Cantwell had already scored out a rectangle that was about a foot deep. For a horse, you went eight. At six, a stubborn coyote might dig. At eight, they'd circle the ground and whine, pissed that they could smell the meat, but knowing that it was not worth their while.

Last summer, whenever he was in the pasture, all Cantwell could hear was the snap of nail guns. Now all he heard was the chirp of the blue jays and the tip of his shovel echoing off the butte.

"What the hell happened?" Lupe asked.

Cantwell pulled the Post-it note apology from his wallet. He handed it to Lupe.

"That absolves everything," Cantwell said. "Right?"

Lupe shook his head and handed back the Post-it note to Cantwell. Lupe had just turned twenty-two, worked weekdays cleaning and detailing at Dennison's Buick dealership in Blood Lake and weekends at the ranch. He was married with a kid. There was another one on the way in a few months. How could someone so young even have a clue that this was the right way to do things?

"Why didn't you use the backhoe?" Lupe asked him. "You trying to stop your heart again?"

"I wanted to sweat," Cantwell said. "And I was pissed. Now I don't know what I am. Mostly sweaty, I guess."

"You want the backhoe down here?" Lupe asked.

Cantwell shook his head no. "This here is what we call environmentally friendly," he said. "We're saving the boss tons of money on his carbon credits."

Lupe got the pickaxe from the truck bed. He tied a rope around his trailer hitch and tossed it into the hole. He hopped down next to Cantwell and began to loosen the rocky ground near where Cantwell was sticking his shovel.

"Dennison heard about this yet?" he asked.

"For all I know, he's the son of a bitch that wrote the dumbass apology," Cantwell said.

After his heart attack, Cantwell had turned into an insomniac. He figured it was partly due to his heart's unstable rhythm and partly because he felt like everything around him seemed to have been pulled away from its moorings.

There was a new town named Whisper Rock, a couple of towns over from the ranch. All the building facades were reproduced to look like a whitewashed version of America. There were draped flags and wraparound porches on all of the houses. It had been done horribly. The one time Cantwell had been to the hardware store to buy a new chainsaw, they didn't have one. The whole town felt creepy and false, calling too much attention to what it tried to mean.

In Cantwell's mind, no one ever recreated the past right. Things like this, the way things were and had been and were not now, this was, as far as Cantwell could tell, even though he knew full well it was a stupid damn thing to ponder, was what kept him up at night. That and sitting there in bed waiting for his heart to explode.

The wind picked up and Cantwell caught a whiff of the dead horse. The smell would soon make its way toward the paddock and the balloon arch. Once it got there no amount of citronella would make it disappear. Cantwell's eyes were pinched and itchy from the dust. He was kept up by the previous night's nuptials. The guests had hooted and hollered underneath his window until late into the night. No matter how loud he turned up the calming ocean sound on that noisemaker that his sister, Lily, had sent him for his last birthday, Cantwell could not fall asleep. After an hour in bed staring at the ceiling, he got up and pushed a chair over to the window and watched everyone dancing below him. He'd tried a window fan before the noisemaker, but the whirring had irritated him—he always thought that he heard voices whispering to him underneath the hum.

"How many guests tonight?" Cantwell asked.

"Two hundred," Lupe told him. "Bride and groom were high school sweethearts or some damn thing."

Cantwell wiped his brow with his shirt. This was where the digging got tough—all hard clay and bitten rock. He stepped on the shovel and it spun away from him and flopped on the ground.

"You sure this isn't deep enough?" Lupe asked.

Cantwell didn't answer him. He picked up the shovel and stuck it back into the earth. He dug until he could only see the sky and the lip of the grave above him and then he told Lupe they were done. Cantwell used the snowplow attached to the front of the truck to push the horse into the grave. Then he pushed all the shoveled dirt back into the hole. When the hole was full he drove the truck back and forth over it to tamp it down.

"You bartending tonight?" he asked Lupe.

"I'm here until this shit ends," Lupe told him.

Cantwell spent the rest of the afternoon running around the ranch putting out the small logistical fires. The florist needed help connecting rose bunches to the balloon arch. The sections of the wedding cake needed to be transferred from the decorator's minivan and into the kitchen's fridge.

"You eat lunch yet?" Purvey asked him. She pulled out a chair from her desk, told him to sit. She placed a sandwich in front of him. She made him low-fat, low-cholesterol meals, something he knew he should eat but, left to his own devices, never did.

"You hear that the police caught a van with a ton of copper from the houses up on the hill the other night?" she asked. Purvey lived in Junction Creek in a small apartment. She had invited Cantwell there for dinner one night. He'd felt her wanting something from him the moment he walked inside the door. It was too small and too warm and she had too big of a smile on her face. After he'd eaten dinner, he had faked a migraine and gotten the hell out of there. She'd invited him a couple of times since, but he'd been ready with excuses.

"Saw it all," he told her. When Cantwell heard the sirens and the flashing lights, he got out his telescope and watched the entire thing play out. The state troopers crouched behind their cars and drew their shotguns on the van and the men filed out of the van with their hands held high above their heads, then the troopers wrestled them to the ground, handcuffed them, and shoved them into their squad cars.

Cantwell ate his sandwich quickly, thanked Purvey. He found Lupe setting up chairs for the ceremony.

"Are the doves ready?" Lupe asked him. "The photographer just asked me."

Cantwell found the photographer in the paddock standing with the bride. The bride was dressed in jeans and a T-shirt, but her hair and makeup were already done. Standing next to her were two blonde girls with their hair in ringlets. They were all clearly sisters. All of them had dress bags draped over their shoulders. They held shoeboxes in their hands.

"We fell in love with this place," the bride told the photographer as she walked into the bridal suite. "After we saw it, there was no other place we wanted."

Usually Cantwell was too busy to watch the ceremony, but since he was responsible for the doves, he dressed in a gray suit and stood in the back. After the vows, when the music for the recessional started, he pulled the latch on the cage and shooed the doves out. He walked over to the dining room and helped finish setting up the tables for dinner. When that was done, Cantwell took three beers from the bar and leaned against the fence and drank.

Just after dinner, the bride came out from the dining room with a glass of champagne. She was walking with her sister. Both of them looked drunk and happy. They moved over and stood near Cantwell. The bride's sister lit a cigarette and drifted over toward the paddock. The bride stood near Cantwell. She smelled like hairspray and cake frosting. There were tiny beads of sweat on her upper lip.

"I had to get away for a couple of minutes, you know?" she said.

The dance had started now and through the windows of the barn Cantwell saw a bunch of young people jumping up and down. It always looked strange to see people moving like this without being able to hear the accompanying music. They looked like they were flailing around without any sort of rhyme or reason.

"I'm doing the same damn thing," he told her.

The girl took a sip of her drink. She reminded him of this woman he'd known before his ex-wife. Some girl he'd met at a bar once in Tulsa who kept on playing the same Steely Dan song on the jukebox over and over.

"You're Jason's uncle, right?" the bride asked.

"Am I?" he said.

"I'm so sorry about your wife," the bride said.

Cantwell paused. He did not know whether or not he should go forward with this lie, but he wanted some company.

"Yes, yes," he said, shifting his gaze toward the ground. "It's been pretty difficult this last little while."

The bride put her arms around him and gave him a hug. She pulled back and took her palm and cupped it around the back of his head. She placed her forehead against his.

"Save a dance for me," she told him.

Cantwell usually called it a night after the dance began. Tonight he did not leave. He leaned against the bar and Lupe kept his gin and tonic full. Dennison had left for the night and the catering manager was working in her office. Cantwell had no clue how many drinks he'd had by now. Ten? Twelve? At some point the bride came over to the bar and pulled him onto the dance floor. She leaned her head on his shoulder and he spun her around. When the song ended, she kissed him on the cheek.

"It'll get better," she told him. "It just takes time."

Cantwell nodded to her, then turned and made his way out through the side door. The dancing had loosed something in his gut and he steadied himself on the aluminum siding of the barn. There was a clear view of the hills from here and he saw that there were more bright lights up there by those houses, more men gutting them of their remaining aluminum and copper. Cantwell wished he was younger and stronger. He wished he had a tank full of gas and a bandolier full of ammo. He wished he still knew some badass motherfuckers.

As he stood there, he felt the salt rise in his throat and he buckled over and puked.

As he stumbled away, Cantwell pulled out his wallet. He went over to the bride and groom's convertible. He stuck the Post-it note to the windshield of their car.

Sorry. It was in that jackass blue glittery handwriting. He stood staring at it. Would the bride even see it? Would someone else pull it off the windshield before they drove away? Would someone think that it was just garbage and crumple it up and toss it into the wind?

Cantwell left the car and moved off toward the creek. The crickets were chirping at a quick enough pace to let him know it was still warm enough to bed down outdoors. He walked until the lights from the ranch fell away then he flopped down in the grass and closed his eyes. He hoped for the bride and groom's convertible to ride down the road soon. He wanted the sound of tin cans clattering down the blacktop. From this far away that sound would not be annoying. He figured it would sound like wind through chimes, something that might help you drift off into a long and uninterrupted sleep.

DUPLEX

When I was thirty-three, my mother died and I had to move out of her rent-free basement. At first I crashed on my brother's couch, but then a bunch of his wife's bras and panties went missing and I got blamed. Next I lived in an apartment above a laundromat but there was a mysterious bra and panty fire in my bedroom and the landlord kicked me out. After the apartment, I rented a room at the Starlite Motel but then my ferret, Stabby, killed the owner's cat. At that point I was running low on cash so I crashed in the backseat of my Corolla. One night I went to a bar for free happy hour tacos and played darts with a man named Jayhole. Jayhole told me he was looking for a new roommate because his old roommate, Dan, had recently passed away.

"Dan fell off a bridge," Jayhole said. "Or maybe he jumped. He didn't leave a suicide note so nobody really knows for sure."

Jayhole was a large man with a barrel chest and a short ponytail that resembled a salt and pepper turd. He'd been a bounty hunter for twenty years but then he'd gotten shot in the kneecap. He walked with a hitch, but he had this wicked cane with a bunch of writhing snakes on the handle that made it look awesome to have a fucked-up leg.

"Do you wanna take a look at Dan's old room?" he asked.

I was five foot eight when I wore my tallest shoes. I weighed 150 pounds when I wore my heaviest coat. I'd recently grown a scraggly Civil War–style beard to hide my weak chin, but people kept on telling me that the beard made my face look even more horsey than it normally did.

"I'd love to," I told Jayhole.

On the way over to his place, Jayhole told me more about himself. He was forty-five years old. He drove a forklift at an office supply store. He'd been divorced twice and had a teenage daughter he hadn't seen in years.

"That's too bad," I told him.

"I heard through the grapevine she's a total bitch," he said, "so no big loss."

I offered up some tidbits about myself. How I sometimes stole steaks from grocery stores and sold them door-to-door from a cooler in my trunk. How I'd recently taken a jewelry-making class and was planning to open a kiosk at the mall to sell some of my mind-blowing earring and necklace designs.

We pulled up in front of a duplex. It was brown stucco and there was a rusted basketball hoop out back. Jayhole lived in the bottom half of the building. He gave me a quick tour of the apartment, the kitchen, the bathroom and its claw-foot tub. In the living room, there was an aquarium with a boa constrictor inside it. There was a piece of paper taped to the aquarium that read "Hi! I'm Strangles."

"We're not supposed to have pets," Jayhole said, "but the landlord is old and he never comes around."

We walked down the hall to Dan's old room. Dan's single bed and his dresser were still sitting there. Some of Dan's old T-shirts, which looked about my size, hung in the closet. The room smelled like incense, not death.

"It's four hundred dollars a month plus utilities," Jayhole told me. "What do you think?"

I quickly weighed the pros and cons. Had I showered in the sink of a Burger King bathroom that morning? Yes. Did my car reek of steak and ferret? Uh-huh. Was I going to die just because the guy who lived here before me died? Probably not.

"It's perfect," I told Jayhole.

For our first few weeks, Jayhole and I got along great. I made him a shark's-tooth necklace and he gave me a punch card from a bagel place that only needed three more punches to get a free sandwich. One night I grilled him a stolen sirloin and he showed me his scrapbook.

Jayhole's bounty hunting scrapbook was full of pictures of him standing next to bail jumpers he'd tracked down over the years. In the pictures, he was always smiling and laughing and the people he'd brought to justice were always frowning and bloody. In some of the pictures, Strangles was draped around Jayhole's neck like a scarf.

"It looks like you loved your work," I told him.

Jayhole stared out the window into our backyard where a stray dog was nosing through a garbage bag. He scratched behind his ear and some flakes of dead skin floated down among the crumbs on the kitchen floor. It wasn't difficult to see Jayhole missed the rush of bounty hunting, that it was his one true calling, that he hadn't found anything that would ever replace its powerful and enticing high.

"I don't want to sound like some sad sack yearning for lost

gridiron glory," he told me, "but those were absolutely the best days of my life."

One night I brought my tackle box of jewelry-making supplies into the kitchen to work on some new broche and stickpin designs. Jayhole saw me sitting there and got his storage tub of pictures and scrapbooking materials. For the rest of the night we worked side by side, him with his glue stick and me with my soldering gun. While we worked, Jayhole told me stories about the people in his scrapbook.

"This guy tried to get away from me by climbing into the ductwork of an auto parts store," he said, pointing to a picture of a man with two swollen eyes and an ear that was partially torn off. "He didn't think I'd go up there after him, but I tossed Strangles up into the vent and that dude jumped down real quick."

Each page of Jayhole's scrapbook held a picture of someone who thought they could outsmart him, who thought they could disappear off the grid. I didn't have any sympathy for these dopes. I often liked to imagine them sipping a piña colada at a beachside bar thinking they'd gotten away scot-free until Jayhole leapt out from behind a palm tree, yelled "Surprise!" and tasered the shit out of them.

While Jayhole showed me some more pictures, the man who lived in the upstairs part of the duplex, Caruso, started to tromp around above us. Caruso was a fat, pasty guy who occasionally deejayed birthday parties and weddings. He had an English accent that disappeared whenever he was angry or drunk. Both Jayhole and I hated him. Whenever Caruso walked around or danced to one of his new mashups our ceiling shook and the pots and pans on our stovetop rattled. Jayhole had spoken to him a number of times about wearing noise-dampening slippers or simply walking around less, but Caruso never listened.

"Stop tromping!" Jayhole yelled up at him through the ceiling. "Stop deejaying, quit making your stupid mashups and dance jams!"

Jayhole took an aluminum tentpole that was sitting next to the refrigerator and he pounded it on the ceiling. A minute later Caruso tromped down the front stairs and into our kitchen.

"Gimme it back," Caruso yelled, poking Jayhole in the chest with his index finger. "Gimme it back right fucking now."

Jayhole handed me his beer and then he reeled back and punched Caruso in the mouth. Caruso tumbled into the radiator.

"Give you what back?" Jayhole asked.

Caruso stood up and bull-rushed Jayhole. Caruso was ugly enough not to care what happened to his face, which was a lucky thing because Jayhole's next punch smashed into Caruso's nose and sent him sprawling back into the wall.

"There was a Tupperware container in my fridge," Caruso said, spitting a rope of blood out onto our linoleum. "And there was a piece of tape with the word 'Aphrodisiac' written on the container. I paid good money for it and I want it back."

I was actually the one who'd stolen Caruso's aphrodisiac. A few days ago, I went upstairs to borrow an egg and found Caruso's apartment door wide open. When I walked inside, I found him passed out on the couch. He didn't have any eggs in his refrigerator so I took the Tupperware container instead. Right now it was hidden in the mini fridge in my room. The aphrodisiac was dark red—it looked like it was mostly made of beets. I knew I should ration it for when I finally found a girlfriend, but I'd started to eat spoonfuls of it before I went to bed because I loved the sex dreams it gave me.

"What do you need it for?" I asked Caruso.

"There's a girl staying with me," he said. "And she likes that sort of thing."

I had a hard time imagining what kind of woman would date pig-nosed Caruso, with his pasty skin and his English accent that kept disappearing and reappearing. I was wondering why I couldn't ever find a woman at any of the bars or apartment buildings where I sold my steaks or why the women who I chatted with online never actually showed up for our dates. As I watched Caruso and Jayhole circle each other, I heard a women's voice call down.

"Caruso," the voice whined. "Hurry up already."

Jayhole stood with his fists raised waiting for Caruso to charge him again, but instead Caruso just shrugged his shoulders, turned, and walked back upstairs.

In July I had a great month selling steaks. I sold them as quickly as I stole them. Some of my regular customers began to make requests for specific cuts of meat and I was more than happy to oblige.

Unfortunately July was also the month that Jayhole lost his job at the office supply warehouse. After an argument with his boss, Jayhole drove his forklift out to the parking lot and gored the side of his boss's car. The cops were called, but Jayhole knew all of them from his bounty hunting days and they let him off with a warning.

"Everyone at work knows when I'm drinking tequila you should keep your distance," Jayhole told me, "but I guess my boss didn't get that memo, did he?"

Jayhole didn't start looking for a new job right away and so he had plenty of time on his hands. Mostly he filled up his hours by seeing which hard lemonades mixed best with which flavored vodkas, but he also spent a lot of free time playing practical jokes on me.

One night he unscrewed the top of our saltshaker and I dumped a mountain of salt all over my chicken salad sandwich.

On my birthday, he hid my wallet underneath the cedar chips in Stabby's cage and I didn't find it for three days. One time Jayhole spread cellophane over our toilet bowl and when I took a piss, the piss bounced right back up onto my jean shorts. Jayhole's laugh was loud, and sometimes after one of his practical jokes he'd slap me hard on the back and shoulders and the next day my back and shoulders would be sore.

"Could you take it easy on the jokes?" I asked.

Jayhole pinched his eyes together, incredulous. He looked shocked I wasn't enjoying his pranks as much as he was.

"Sure," he told me. "I had no idea they were bothering you."

I went to bed that night hopeful Jayhole would stop his practical joking, but the next morning I woke up and found he'd filled my car up with microwave popcorn and lured some squirrels and pigeons inside the car to eat the popcorn and claw and peck the shit out of my dashboard and bucket seats. Jayhole was watching the proceedings from a lawn chair in our front yard, laughing his ass off.

"Dan didn't get my sense of humor right away either," he told me, "but after a while he thought everything I did was hilarious. You'll come around just like Dan did."

Inside my car, a pigeon squawked at one of the squirrels. I wondered if the birds and squirrels would leave after the popcorn was gone or if they'd hunker down and try to make my car their home.

"Just get a broom and shoo them away," Jayhole said. "They won't put up a fight unless they're rabid."

Before I got the broom, one of the pigeons took a watery shit in my glove compartment. Lately, I'd thought a lot about moving out, but I'd recently taken all the profits from my steak stealing and sunk them into expensive glass beads I was planning to use for my fall jewelry collection. If I was going to move, I needed a few months to scrape together some money for a security deposit.

A few weeks later, Jayhole started to inject horse steroids into his bad knee. He'd gotten them from a friend who was a trainer at the racetrack. His back acne got immediately worse, but his knee started to feel much better. One day, Jayhole woke up and his knee pain was gone. He tossed his cane into the closet and decided it was time he opened his own bounty hunting agency.

"I've gotta be my own boss," he explained. "At this point in my life, I'm too set in my ways to answer to another douchebag in a suit and tie."

To get his body in shape for the grind of bounty hunting, Jayhole lifted weights in our garage. He did yoga, sometimes naked, sometimes not, in our living room.

"I just need a little start-up money to open up shop," he told me. "I just need a couple of bucks to buy tasers and tear gas. I'm not asking for much, but every single person I hit up for money tells me no."

I knew exactly what Jayhole was talking about. I was having the same problem getting my jewelry kiosk off the ground. Over the last month I'd asked my relatives for seed money, but no one would help. Most of them gave me bullshit excuses like, "I just got arrested for vehicular homicide," or, "I finally decided to start paying my child support." The rest of them were shocked that I had the balls to hit them up for money after all the meat and lingerie I'd stolen from them over the years.

"I'm trying to remain positive," Jayhole said, "but it's damn hard."

It was hard. So far I'd invested hundreds of hours designing my fall collection, but I knew no one gave a shit. When I'd started making jewelry I had visions of hot women handing me cold flutes of champagne, dreams of gold-toothed rappers stopping by my kiosk and begging me to design them diamond-crusted crucifixes. None of that had happened yet. I still did my visualization exercises to help make these things happen, but remaining positive was getting difficult. At the swap meet each weekend, I laid my piece of black velvet across my card table and spread out my wares, but almost everyone walked by my booth without breaking stride. On the rare occasion someone stopped, they laughed at my jewelry like it was some sort of gag gift.

"Keep plugging away," I told Jayhole, placing my hand gently on his shoulder. "Don't listen to the naysayers. Our passion to our craft is the only thing that matters."

Jayhole must've appreciated what I'd told him because after I said this he pulled me into his arms and locked me in a bear hug. He held me there for a long time, squeezing my head into his chest. When he let me go, I saw there were tears in his eyes.

"You're the only one who understands," he said.

I knew the horse steroids were giving him crazy mood swings, but from what I could tell his gratitude seemed genuine. Maybe Jayhole just needed some time to trust me? Maybe these jokes he played on me masked some sort of unresolved inner pain? Maybe everything would be wonderful between us from this point forward?

Later that evening, Jayhole broke into my room and wrote the word "Fuckstick" on Stabby's fur in purple marker. He also took a scissors and cut cock-and-ball-shaped holes in all of my T-shirts.

While I scrubbed the marker off Stabby, I thought about disassembling all my jewelry and selling the stones for scrap so I could get enough money together to move out. I got out a pliers, but I just couldn't tear everything apart; I didn't want to give up yet. In the end, I decided the best plan of attack to survive the next few weeks was to avoid Jayhole as much as possible. To make it harder for Jayhole to keep tabs on me, I started to climb in and out of my room through my window. When I was inside my room, I used a flashlight and moved around slowly, trying to not make my floorboards creak. At first I had a hard time adjusting to the darkness, but soon I became proficient at eating soup from a bowl I couldn't see and pissing into a Snapple bottle using only the faint light of the moon.

One night, I heard Jayhole out in the hall doing some push-ups. I was paranoid he'd heard me moving around in my room so I slid underneath my bed to hide. As I lay there among the dust, I noticed a manila envelope taped to the bed frame with the words "Dan's Suicide Note" written on it. I ripped it open.

"To whom it may concern," the note inside said, "I'm killing myself because my roommate Jayhole is driving me insane. He keeps playing horrible pranks on me and every time I try to move out he tracks me down and brings me back here. It's like some demented game to him. I've tried to escape a number of times over the last year, but he won't let me leave."

I must have ripped open the envelope too loudly because the next thing I knew Jayhole burst into my room, grabbed on to my ankle, and yanked me out from under my bed.

"What's this?" he asked, snatching Dan's note out of my hand.

"I found it while I was cleaning," I lied, "but I hadn't gotten a chance to read it yet."

Jayhole read Dan's note and then he crumpled it into a ball. He took his lighter from his pocket and lit it on fire and then he dropped it onto my floor and stood over it while it burned. The fire alarm in the hall went off, but Jayhole yelled over it. "That Dan," he bellowed, "that guy really had a bizarre sense of humor, didn't he?"

That night, after Jayhole left for his dart league, I put Stabby in his carrier and packed my suitcase. I was planning to sleep in my Corolla that night. The next morning, I'd go to a laundromat and steal some newer bras and panties to give to my sister-in-law as a peace offering. I hoped this would be enough for her to let me crash on their couch again.

I loaded Stabby into the trunk first. When I walked back to get my suitcase, Jayhole popped up from the azaleas. He was dressed all in black and his face was painted camouflage. Strangles was draped around his shoulders. I ran to my car, but before I got there, Jayhole shot me in the neck with a blow dart. My hands went numb and I dropped my keys. My knees went sideways and I toppled over into the shrubs.

"I didn't think I put enough tranquilizer on that blow dart," Jayhole said as he stood over me, his head blocking out the moon, "but watching the way you fell, I might have used too much, huh?"

Even though my eyes were having trouble focusing, I could tell Jayhole was excited about catching me. His eyes were open wide and his nostrils were flared. I tried to yell for help, but my tongue wouldn't cooperate. Jayhole set Strangles down on the ground beside me and I felt him curl around my calf. Even though I was scared shitless, I couldn't keep my eyes open.

In the morning, I woke up handcuffed to my bedframe. Jayhole stood across my room from me, flipping through a batch of earrings I'd recently made. I heard Caruso's music upstairs, the heavy bass of his speakers pounding through the ceiling and into my chest. Jayhole's scrapbook was sitting on the floor. There was a new picture of me pasted in it. When he saw I was awake, he walked over and pressed his boot into my stomach.

"What you need to understand," he said, "is that no matter where you go, I'll find you."

He pressed his foot down harder, making it difficult to breathe.

"Now you say it," he told me.

I thought about Dan and his suicide note. I understood how awesome it might have felt for him to jump from that bridge and fly through the air for a few seconds before he hit that water. How wonderful those precious moments of freedom probably felt before his face smashed into the river and his nose got pushed up into his brain and everything went black and Jayholeless.

"No matter where I go, you'll always find me," I repeated.

Jayhole bent down and unlocked the handcuffs. Then he went out into the kitchen and fried up one of my stolen steaks. I curled up under my covers. I listened to the bass of Caruso's dance mix, ooontz, ooontz, ooontz, pounding over and over, never stopping, never ceasing. The pounding sounded so close it felt like it was happening right inside my stupid head.

II

Maybe it was Stockholm Syndrome kicking in, but over the next few weeks I learned to accept my situation with Jayhole. Like most abductees, I started to focus on the positive aspects of my current living situation. I had a roof over my head, didn't I? Other people certainly had problems with their roommates too, didn't they? Numerous scientific studies have proven that humans can get used to just about anything as long as they maintain proper perspective, right?

By now Jayhole had started to ask me to do him an occasional favor. Doing his laundry or helping him steal a Labradoodle from his ex-girlfriend's yard. That kind of thing. I did these favors without asking too many questions because Jayhole asked me not to ask too many questions as a personal favor to him.

One day Jayhole asked me to run to the liquor store to get him a case of beer. When I got back with the beer, Jayhole wasn't home and there was a strange man passed out on our kitchen floor. The man's long black beard was knotted around our radiator. Besides being beardtied to our radiator, there was a balled tube sock stuffed into the man's mouth and his hair had been cut in an unflattering way. The word "SHIT" had been written in capital letters on his forehead.

"Did Jayhole do this to you?" I asked the man. "Are you another one of his jokes?"

The man removed the tube sock from his mouth.

"I'm looking for my wife," he told me.

The man was about my age and I could tell from the tone of his voice he was very tired of saying this particular sentence. I could tell that he'd said it too many times and now he wanted to say something different or better. The man tried to struggle to his feet. I warned him to stay down, but he got halfway up before the skin on his face pulled taut and he made a sound that reminded me of when Jayhole and I were down by the river and Jayhole kept hitting that muskrat over and over with that golf club.

"You're beardtied," I explained to him. "You're beardtied good."

The man slumped back down to the kitchen floor. I noticed he had a tattoo of a Jesus fish on his left arm. His fish had claw marks on it though, like he'd tried to scratch it away. I wanted to tell him about how Jayhole had recently beardtied me to the handle of his van, about how I had learned my lesson about beards. I wanted to tell the man that while the finely trimmed goatee I now wore might look dapper and sophisticated, it was mostly for safety.

The man was jerking his head back and forth to see if he could pull himself free, but this was useless; his beard was really knotted, he was wasting his energy. I handed him my pocketknife.

"It's the only way," I said.

The man's beard was a thoughtful beard, something you could

tell he took great pride in. It wasn't something that had occurred because of laziness or because he'd lost a bet on a college football game. He tried to get his fingernail inside the knot, but that was not going to work either.

The man soon stopped pulling. Then he picked up my knife and started to saw. When he'd finished, I handed him a beer. He gulped it down. His beard was a jagged mess now, totally ruined. I could see the wheels turning in his head. It was starting to come back to him, how he'd arrived here, who'd done this horrible injustice. I was expecting him to yell out Jayhole's name, but instead he shook his fist and yelled, "Caruso!"

The man's name was Harley. He said he'd driven here to win his wife Erica back from Caruso but then Caruso had jumped him from behind and bonked him on the head with a lead pipe or a baseball bat, he did not know which.

As we talked, I heard the front door open and Jayhole walked into the kitchen.

"This looks like a fun time," he said, noting the knot of beard around the radiator. "This looks like a fun time indeed."

I popped open a beer for Jayhole, explained how I'd thought that Harley was one of his practical jokes, but then found out that Caruso was responsible.

"Christ," Jayhole said. "Beardtying is my move. Isn't anything sacred anymore?"

Harley pulled out a worn picture of Erica from his wallet and pushed it across the kitchen table. In the picture, she was wearing a skirt. She had incredibly curvy calves, calves that I could only think about running my tongue, slowly, up and down, over and over again. I'd long imagined finding a woman who would let me do this to her body without charging me premium prices, but I hadn't found one yet.

While we sat there, we heard Caruso start to tromp around above us. The overhead light rattled and the dishes in our kitchen cabinets bumped together. The saltshaker on the table tipped over.

"Is he jumping rope up there?" Harley asked. "Or doing step aerobics?"

"That's just his normal walking," I explained.

"That's incredibly noisy normal walking," Harley said.

Jayhole took off his boot and chucked it at the ceiling, but that didn't do anything to make Caruso stop. Soon Jayhole stormed out to the garage. When he came back he was holding a chainsaw.

"What's that for?" I asked, but Jayhole didn't answer me. He walked into my room and climbed up on top of my bed. He started up the chainsaw. As he revved the engine, my room filled with blue smoke. Harley and I moved under the doorjamb and watched as Jayhole shoved the chainsaw into my ceiling. Chunks of plaster and wood rained down onto my jewelry table and bedroom floor. When the dust finally cleared, there was a hole in my ceiling. Caruso's head quickly popped through it.

"What in the fuck?" he yelled down. "Are you crazy?"

"The girl comes down here now," Jayhole yelled up.

"No, no, no," Caruso said. "No way in hell. The girl stays put."

"This here is her husband," Jayhole said, motioning to Harley. "And he wants to talk to her."

Caruso's head disappeared and I heard him discussing the situation with Erica. Before this, whenever I'd climbed up on my bed to eavesdrop on them everything was muffled. I couldn't hear their conversations clearly and I could never tell if they were moaning in pain or moaning sexually. The hole in the ceiling made the acoustics wonderful; you could hear everything they were saying like they were whispering it right into your ear.

"You stay here," Erica said to Caruso. "I'll handle this."

Erica walked down the front stairs and into my room. Her hair was ratty and her face was so-so, but her calves looked even more buxom in real life than in the picture Harley had shown us. At first she held out her arms to Harley like she was going to give him a hug, but when he stepped closer, she clocked him. It was a good punch and Harley fell to the ground.

"We're done," she yelled down at him. "We're finished. I've told you that a hundred times already, but I guess you needed to hear it again?"

Erica stormed upstairs. I knelt down next to Harley. There was a small river of blood sliding out of his mouth and down into the neck of his sweater. His eye was swollen and the word on his forehead was smudged. You could still make out the "S" and the "H" pretty well, but the "I" and the "T" were really hard to read.

III

The next morning I found that Caruso had covered the hole in my ceiling with an area rug. Unfortunately, whenever he or Erica walked around upstairs plaster dust rained into my room. I wiped things down constantly, but there always seemed to be a new layer of dust covering everything. While I wiped down my mini fridge, there was a knock on the door. When I opened it I found Harley standing there.

"What would it cost me to sit in your room and listen to Erica walk above me?" he asked.

The skin under Harley's left eye was ringed purple and one of his nostrils was swollen shut, but he'd already heeded my advice and shaved off his beard. I could tell that the skin underneath it hadn't seen sunlight in a long time. His forehead and nose were leathery while the rest of his face had a grayish, waxy look.

"How about twenty bucks an hour?" I said.

I didn't expect to get this amount, but Harley dug into his wallet and pulled out forty bucks without complaint. I cleared off a recliner for him and he sat down. He pulled a six-pack from his bag and held out a can to me.

It didn't seem worth it to me, to pay to interact with his wife in such a limited way, sometimes not at all, but Harley didn't seem to mind. He kept stopping by, a couple times a week, sitting in my recliner while his ex-wife walked overhead.

One morning, I woke up to Erica staring down at me from the hole in my ceiling. Her legs were dangling into my room. She kicked them back and forth and then she crossed her calves, one over the other. She massaged her right calf with her big toe, slowly kneading it. I felt the blood rush to my cheeks.

"Is that you I heard crying the other night?" she asked.

It was me, but it wasn't really crying. A couple of nights ago I'd gotten home and found that Jayhole had turned all the furniture in my room upside down. My bed, my desk, my jewelry table, everything. What came out of my mouth then was more of a low-pitched wail. There were hardly any tears at all.

I wondered how long Erica had been watching me sleep. I'd started to sleepwalk recently. A few weeks ago Jayhole had found me in the kitchen spreading mustard all over my chest. Another time I woke up sitting on top of our refrigerator, naked and hunched over like a gargoyle. I suspected it might be a side effect of the aphrodisiac but hell if I was going to stop taking it.

"Maybe I could help you with Jayhole," Erica said. "Stop him from bullying you."

"I don't think that's a good idea," I told her.

The last time I'd tried to escape from Jayhole was the time he beardtied me to the door handle of his van and drove off around our neighborhood. I kept up with him for a block before I fell, but he kept dragging me for another block to teach me a lesson.

I knew by now that it was better to laugh off his jokes, to play along, to not try to escape. Maybe one of us would die soon and maybe that person would be Jayhole.

"I know you stole Caruso's aphrodisiac," Erica told me. "I saw you eating some of it."

I thought about the sex dream I had last night. How I got swallowed by a whale, but how there was a woman with large floppy breasts inside of the whale and then how we ended up screwing right on top of the whale's tongue. It was wet and exciting. These sex dreams were the only thing keeping me sane right now. There was no way I was giving this aphrodisiac back.

"I don't know what you think you saw," I told Erica, "but I don't have the aphrodisiac."

Erica moved her legs out of the hole. A few seconds later a ladder slid down into my room. She climbed down the rungs and walked over to my mini fridge. She took out the Tupperware container of aphrodisiac and swallowed a spoonful of it and then scrambled back up the ladder. I was too shocked to do anything about it.

"Thanks!" she yelled down.

I heard Erica moaning a little while later. She hadn't put the rug over the top of the hole to muffle the sound at all. I could hear everything clearly, which I thought was pretty neighborly of her.

The next day Caruso and Erica got into a huge fight. I'd just returned home after I'd shoplifted some fancy grass-fed steaks from the co-op. I took the aluminum tentpole from the kitchen and pushed the area rug away from the hole so I could hear them better.

"Where were you last night while I was deejaying the Rosales wedding?" Caruso asked her.

"I told you already," Erica said. "Jill and I went shopping."

"That's sounds like fun," he said, "except I called Jill and she told me she hasn't seen you in a month."

"You checked up on me?" Erica said.

"Now we're even," Caruso told her.

"Fuck if we're even," Erica said, "we're never going to be even."

Sometimes during their fights, Erica mentioned something hurtful that Caruso had done to her recently, some mysterious and horrible thing, but she never mentioned exactly what that thing was. All I knew is that she wasn't going to probably forgive or forget whatever it was anytime soon.

"Jesus Christ," Caruso said. "Can't we ever just move on? Haven't I done enough penance?"

Erica yelled "No!" and threw a vase at him. The vase shattered against the wall and a river of water and glass cascaded through the hole in my ceiling and onto my floor.

"I can smell the aphrodisiac on your breath," Caruso yelled. "Were you the one who stole it? To use with someone else?"

Caruso rifled through the drawers of their apartment, dumping their contents out. Erica picked up a coffee cup and threw it at him. It smashed apart and some of the coffee started to drip down into my room.

"You don't know what the fuck you are talking about," Erica yelled. "You don't know the first goddamn thing."

Soon Caruso ran down the front stairs, got into his car, and drove off. After he was gone, Erica's legs slid down into the hole in my ceiling. I was busy sweeping up the chards from the vase.

"Can you believe that shit?" she asked. "Can you believe he's so controlling?"

Erica slid her ladder down into my room. I watched her legs as she descended the rungs. Had her calves gotten more buxom over the last few days? Was she doing toe raises to pump them up? She stepped off the last rung and went over and opened the door of my mini fridge and took another spoonful of the aphrodisiac and swallowed it. This time, instead of immediately climbing back up the ladder, she took another spoonful and carried it across the room and put it up to my lips.

"This is a one-time thing," she said, pushing me down onto my bed and straddling me.

When Harley stopped by later that day I was busy making Erica a pendant. It had a smaller heart inside a bigger heart. There were some small pink stones filling the smaller heart. The pendant was meant to be worn below the knee and above the ankle. I called it a calflet. It was one of the most sensual pieces of jewelry I'd ever made and I was excited to see Erica's reaction to it when I draped it over her mid-leg.

"It smells like sex in here," Harley said.

I felt a little guilty about what had happened between Erica and I, but not enough to tell Harley. Erica had been a generous lover, letting me run my tongue over her calves for a very long time and she hadn't looked at me like I was a creep when I finished. She told me that I shouldn't fall in love with her, but I was having a hard time doing anything but.

"That's just Stabby," I told Harley. "It's his glands."

Harley sat down in my desk chair. He'd brought a cooler full of beer with him and he passed one to me. We clinked bottles in a toast.

"To love," Harley said.

"It's great, isn't it?" I said.

While we sat there Caruso and Erica started to yell at each other again. Caruso was asking her where the aphrodisiac was and Erica was denying she had it.

"They've been fighting like that a lot lately," I said.

Obviously Harley enjoyed hearing this. I was happy too, thinking about how Caruso would probably storm off after their fight and then how Harley would leave and then how Erica would slide her legs down the hole into my room. After we made love we'd open a bottle of wine and fry up a few grass-fed steaks.

Soon though, the fighting between Caruso and Erica softened and we heard giggling. After that, soul music began to flow out of Caruso's speakers and we heard some lusty laughter and then Erica began to lightly moan over the bumping of the bass and then Caruso began to grunt in an erotic way and next there was some skin on skin flapping sounds that coincided with the rhythm of the soul music and then the moaning and grunting got louder and the skin slapping sounds got more urgent.

Harley covered up his ears. I wanted to do that too, but I thought if did it might give away the fact I'd slept with Erica so I just listened to each one of Caruso's thrusts like it was no big deal, like I didn't care one bit.

When Caruso and Erica finished, I motioned to Harley that he could uncover his ears. Except they weren't actually done. There was a short period of rest but then Caruso put on a different record with heavier bass and quicker drumbeats and then everything started up again, the moaning, the flapping, even louder than before.

"I'm going to get some fresh air," Harley told me, but I could tell he was done for today, that he might not come back ever again.

I tried to distract myself from the noise upstairs by dusting, but it was hard to concentrate. It sounded like Caruso and Erica were boning right next to my ear. It was also hard to listen to them because it sounded like Erica was having much more fun fucking Caruso than she'd had fucking me. I looked up into the hole to see if I could see any sex shadows or stray feet, but every time I looked up a bunch of plaster dust fell into my eyes.

Soon Jayhole stopped by my room to see what the racket was. While Jayhole and I stood there, we heard a cracking sound. When I looked up I saw that a hairline crack on the ceiling had grown into a small chasm. It was growing wider with each one of Caruso's thrusts.

"Move!" Jayhole yelled as he pulled me under the doorjamb as the ceiling collapsed and Erica and Caruso fell through the air and landed on my floor with a loud thump.

Jayhole and I waded through the mess of wood and plaster. Erica had some cuts on her face, but she looked all right. She'd been riding on top of Caruso and hadn't taken the brunt of the fall. Caruso didn't look good. He was just lying there, his mouth open, his neck twisted in a strange way, blood trickling out of his ear.

"That doesn't look good," Jayhole said. "That doesn't look good at all."

IV

The next night Erica knocked on my door. Her face was bruised and one of her feet was in a walking boot. I'd spent most of the day returning my room back to normal, carting the plaster and lath to the garbage can. It was still a mess but I cleared a spot for her on my recliner.

"Caruso's awake now," she told me. "But both of his legs are broken and his neck is all messed up."

Erica walked back into her bedroom. I heard her pull the covers over her head.

While she was sleeping, I got the ladder from the garage and I snuck into her apartment. I didn't want to do anything too creepy, so I just sat by her bedside watching her breathe in and out. After I'd had enough of that, I tied the calflet onto her leg and climbed back down into my room.

The next morning Jayhole needed me to run a couple of errands for him. While I was out, he went into my room and dumped out a bag of marshmallows on my rug. It was a hot day and they melted into the shag.

"That's going to be really hard to clean up," Jayhole cackled. "Way harder than I thought. Wow. Sorry."

In the last few days, Jayhole had given up on the idea to start his own bounty hunting business. No one would lend him the start-up money.

"The universe is trying to tell me something," he said. "I was deaf to it for a while, but now I can hear what it is saying."

I wondered if I should quit making jewelry too. At the swap meet last weekend, no one had even stopped by my table to look at what I was selling. Was this the universe telling me something too? If no one really cares what you make, what's the point of working so damn hard on it?

I picked at some of the marshmallow slurry in my rug with a fork. When I tried to pull it out it left a bald spot. The rug was ruined and I rolled it up and hauled it out to the garbage.

"That sucks," Erica said from upstairs. "That's not cool to do that kind of shit to another human being."

Erica had just showered and her wet hair hung around her shoulders. She was wearing a pair of shorts and the calflet was draped enticingly over her leg.

"Thanks for the gift," she said, pointing to her calflet, "but I told you the other day was a one-time thing, okay?"

"Maybe you could let our one-time thing be a two-time thing or four- or nine-time thing?" I asked.

"How about I help you get revenge on Jayhole instead?" she asked.

"I don't think you can help with that," I said. "I don't think anyone can."

"I can help you," she said. "Caruso left me some information I can use."

I shook my head no. "Let's just leave well enough alone," I said.

"Has Harley been coming over?" Erica asked. "Was he in your room before the ceiling fell?"

"He comes over to listen to you walk around above him," I said.

When I told her this, I noticed a softening around Erica's eyes. Her mouth curled into a quick smile. I could tell she was remembering something good that Harley had done for her once. I could tell she was rooting around in her file of Harley memories and she was wondering if whatever had gone wrong between them could be patched up.

"That sounds like something he would do," she said.

Later that day, Harley knocked on my door. Erica had gone to the hospital to visit Caruso.

"She's not here," I told him. "She might not be back for a while."

Harley held out two twenties.

"I'll chance it," Harley said.

I went and walked around my neighborhood for about an hour to give Harley some privacy. When I got back to my room, Erica's ladder was lying on my floor and my bed sheets were twisted and half of the aphrodisiac was gone. There was a padded envelope sitting on top of Stabby's cage. I opened it and two pairs of panties fell out on the floor.

"Harley and I patched things up," the note said. "We're going to give it another go. Here are a couple of things to add to your collection. Tomorrow, you'll receive an even better present from me."

V

When I got up the next morning, I found two women, one old and one young, clearly mother and daughter, sitting on the kitchen floor. They both had the same color eyes and the same pursed lips and they had both tied their long hair in a knot around our radiator. They were sharing a bag of potato chips, passing it back and forth.

"Who are you?" I asked.

"We're not leaving until we see Jayhole," the older one said.

"We're sitting right here until we talk to that delinquent bastard," the younger one said."He owes us a ton of child support."

"Thousands of dollars' worth," the older woman said.

"Lots of zeroes," the younger one said. "Time for him to pay up."

Soon Jayhole walked into the kitchen to make himself breakfast. He'd just gotten out of the shower and was wearing his robe. When he saw the two women sitting on the floor, he jumped backward.

"Oh, hell no," he screamed. "No goddamn way."

"We thought that's what you'd say," the younger one said.

"Those exact words," the older one said.

"Unfortunately we know you too well," the younger one said.

"Too bad for us," the older one said.

"Too bad for us indeed," the younger one said.

Jayhole stood across the room from them. The younger one had Jayhole's nose and his scratchy voice and she seemed to be taking great satisfaction in someone else's unease in the same exact way Jayhole liked to do.

"Damn," she told him, "you've really gotten fat."

Jayhole cinched the belt of his robe tighter. I poured a bowl of cereal and sat down at the kitchen table to watch.

"Now that we found you," the older one said, "we're not leaving here until you pay up."

"How the hell did you find me?" Jayhole asked.

"You were fucking easy to find," the older woman said. "We have our ear to the ground and people hate you."

"So damn easy," the younger one said. "You've got tons of enemies."

Jayhole ran to his room and I heard him ranting to himself about how unfair this was, how this was bullshit, that a mistake he'd made twenty years ago was still haunting his ass.

"Same old Jayhole," the older one said.

"Same old Jayhole," the younger one said. "He'll pack his bags tonight and disappear, but then we'll track him down in a few months and fuck up his life again."

I chatted with the ladies for the rest of the morning. I found out their names were Julie and Lisa and that they'd driven here from Ohio when they'd gotten the tip about Jayhole's location from Erica. While we talked, we heard Jayhole packing up his possessions. He carried the aquarium with Strangles in it down the hall and outside. Soon we heard his van peel out.

"He won't ever pay up," Lisa said. "So we like to track him once every six months to mess up his life."

"That's the fun part of it," Julie said. "We love doing that to him. It's like our hobby now. We plan our vacations around tracking him down. We've seen a lot of the country this way."

Soon Julie and Lisa untied their hair from the radiator and I gave them a tour of the house and introduced them to Stabby. While they were in my room, they looked over some of my new spring jewelry collection. A lot of it they didn't like, but some of it they did. They bought a couple of pairs of earrings for themselves, a necklace for one of their friends. It wasn't much, but it was what I needed right then, a small victory, something to build on, something that told me I was on the right track.

LILY AND ANNABELLE

In March, Lily and Annabelle's dad cheats on their mom with a landscape painter named Fern Greenwald. When their mom finds out, she pushes their father out of the window of their second-floor apartment. Their dad lands on his back in the muddy ground near the bike rack and starts to moan.

Earlier that week, Annabelle found a walkie-talkie on top of a garbage can. As she and Lily run down the fire escape, Annabelle gives a trucker named Rascal the play-by-play.

"My dad just fell out of the window and we're going to see if he's okay," Annabelle tells Rascal.

Lily stands over her father and watches his chest rise and fall. Annabelle bumps her rain boot against her dad's ribs until he opens his eyes.

"Jesus Christ," he tells them. "I could've died."

It's spring and there's mud everywhere and where there isn't mud there are mountains of dirty snow leftover by the plow. Their mother sticks her head out of the apartment window above them. She's holding a big beer glass shaped like a boot in her hand and she motions the girls out of the way and she chucks the beer glass at their dad. It nails him in the shin and he grabs his leg and rolls around on the ground, screaming.

"Now my mom threw a beer stein at my dad and it hit him in the leg and my dad yelled 'fuck,'" Annabelle tells Rascal.

Their dad has been homeschooling the two of them, so the next morning, their mom drives them back to Longwater Community School. Their mom hates Longwater. She hates all the teachers there. She hates the curriculum. She especially hates the principal. Last year she drove over to the principal's house in the middle of the night and dumped a bucket of red paint onto the hood of the principal's car. Their mom believes that there's asbestos in the classroom ceiling tiles even though the principal showed her the paperwork that said all the asbestos in the building was disposed of ten years ago. Their mom's hatred of Longwater doesn't matter anymore, it's been trumped by her anger at their dad. She's bringing the girls back to Longwater for revenge. She's re-enrolling them there because their father hates the school even more than she does.

"This is crap," Annabelle tells her mom as they drive there. "Quit using us as pawns."

Annabelle cut her own hair last night. The bangs are okay, but there's a large bald spot on the top. Both she and Lily are wearing their old uniforms, their blue polo shirts and their khaki pants, but Annabelle has taken a marker and drawn a dragon on her forearm.

"Your dad made you into pawns," their mother says. "Not me."

Lily and Annabelle have been gone from Longwater for four months. When their parents pulled them out of school, their dad bought two old desks and an overhead projector at the Goodwill.

He painted one of the walls in the apartment with chalkboard paint. He printed multiplication worksheets off the Internet. He let them read whatever they wanted to read. He taught them practical things, like how to bake sourdough bread and how to change the oil of a car.

As they drive to the school, Lily remembers when her father was new again. How he returned to live with them after five years of being gone, how he talked to their mom on the phone every night for three months convincing her to take him back. One morning, Lily woke up and their dad was standing at the stove with his mother's pink robe wrapped around him.

"Who wants pancakes?" he asked.

Lily ran right over and hugged him, but Annabelle stood her ground until her mom pushed her across the room and into his arms.

Lily and Annabelle walk down the halls of Longwater, looking at what her old classmates have done since they left. Taped on the walls are self-portraits rendered in beans and pasta shells. In the showcase by the principal's office there are shoe-box dioramas that depict the battles of Bunker Hill and Bull Run. Today the entire school smells like ass, which means lunch is either grilled cheese or pizza.

"Oh, you two," their old teacher, Ms. Marcellus, says when the principal ushers them into the classroom. "I thought you two were *long* gone."

The girls find they've lost their desks. The school supplies they left behind were shoved into a greasy paper bag and stored underneath the radiator. Ms. Marcellus hands the bag to Annabelle, scans the room for a place for them to sit.

"We're out of desks," she tells them. "For now you two are going to need to make your laps into desks."

The girls don't know how to transform a part of their body into something that it isn't. They sit in the back of the classroom by the dead geraniums and the bin of construction paper scrap. Lily pulls her long hair in front of her eyes and twists it into thick ropes while Ms. Marcellus shows them how to divide fractions. Their pencils smell like fried chicken and they're slick and hard to hold.

When they go outside at recess their classmates want to be reminded of how, if they aren't twins, they are in the same grade.

"Beginning of September," Annabelle says, pointing to herself. "End of June," she says, pointing to Lily.

Their mom eats meat, then she pukes meat up. Their father is a vegetarian and when he moved in they had all become vegetarians too. Now that he's moved out, their mom eats *only* meat. Roasts, back bacon, turkey burgers. There aren't any vegetables in the crisper now, only teriyaki jerky.

When their mom pukes, Lily holds her mom's hair to keep it from falling in the toilet. She massages her neck. Today when it happens, she hears Annabelle talking on her walkie-talkie in the other room.

"My mom needs constant attention," she tells a trucker named Jon-Jon. "And she loves drama. It's not hard to figure out why my dad left."

Yesterday, after she bought a pound of chuck, a butcher at the grocery store asked their mom out. His name is Jerry and while their mother doesn't think Jerry was all that cute, he looked stable so she said yes.

"Let's hope you two never have to compromise," she tells them as she primps for the date. "Let's pray that the first one you marry is the right one."

Last night, their dad limped in and dumped his sock drawer into a duffel bag. He slid his lighter off the top of the dresser and dropped it into the pocket of his pants. Their mom sat on the couch and paged through a magazine, trying to care less.

"I brought your children back to Longwater," she told him. "My theory is that any place you hate is the perfect place for us."

Their dad ignored their mom. He grabbed his bag and limped downstairs to the storage space. He held his hip as he walked, cupped the bone like there was something inside there that was going to spill out. Lily and Annabelle watched as he rolled his bike into a blue van.

"When she pushed me out that window I could have fallen someplace hard and not gotten up," he said. "Your mother doesn't understand that. No matter what I did wrong, I didn't deserve that."

When Lily and Annabelle go back upstairs, they find their mom kneeling down by the toilet again. Their bathroom door broke a few months ago and now the door is a green and brown afghan. She and Annabelle watch their mom's head bob up and down through the holes.

"It just keeps coming," she tells them. "You'd think I would be empty but I'm not."

It's Easter week and Lily thinks about how she wants to have a baby named Lazarus. She likes names with z's, names that are not common. She wonders what her life will be like in ten years. She's ten now and when she sits on the swings on the playground and drags her feet on the ground, she wants to know what happens when you double the amount of time you've been on this earth. She understands she's doubled the amount of time she's been on this earth before, that every second is the double of some other second.

Annabelle runs over to the swings and shows Lily her hands. She has poked a stick into her palms and they're bleeding. The other kids see the blood and crowd around.

"Let us look," a boy named Oliver says.

"This is only for my sister to see," Annabelle tells them. "She's the only one who needs to know."

Oliver grabs Annabelle's shoulder and pulls her to face him. Annabelle kicks her knee into his gut and he doubles over.

"Anyone else?" Annabelle asks.

Their dad starts to call them regularly on Thursday nights. Annabelle will not talk to him, but Lily will. One Thursday when he calls, Lily hears someone playing the piano in the background. With the music behind his words, everything he says sounds like a sad song.

"I wish I was there," he tells her. "I wish it wasn't the way it was."

This is the opposite of what their mom tells Lily and Annabelle—she tells them their father doesn't want to be here, that he shacked up with a tramp who can't paint and whose real name is not Fern, but Tammy. Her mother tells Lily that their father will have to live with Tammy when her tits sag and her ass flattens and her neck skin chickens and that stupid leopard-print coat of hers pills and frays.

"What's that music in the background?" Lily asks him.

Her dad says it's just the radio, but Lily can tell it's not good enough. It's off-kilter with songs that never finish. It's too loud in some spots and too soft in others.

"It's not the radio," Lily tells him.

"It's the radio," her dad says.

For Easter dinner, Jerry brings over a glazed ham. Their mother has cleaned all day, down on her hands and knees, scrubbing the hardwood floors. Lily and Annabelle run wild, in and out of the bathroom, through the blanket door.

"Outside," their mom yells at them, "Jerry's gotta piss."

The girls go out on the fire escape, but instead of waiting, Annabelle heads down the stairs and past the dumpster.

"Where are you going?" Lily yells.

Annabelle's talking on her walkie-talkie with a trucker named Herc.

"I'm running away," Lily hears her tell Herc. "Had enough, you know?"

"I hear you," Herc tells her.

Annabelle walks down the white line of the road. Lily follows behind her in the gravel of the ditch. Lily sees a dead fish lying there, then a bike without any wheels. There's a torn-up mattress and small birds keep flying in and out of its guts.

"Where are we going?" Lily asks when Annabelle turns into a neighborhood. Annabelle does not answer her, she walks for another block and then she turns up the sidewalk and pounds on the door of a gray house. A woman opens the door. She's wearing a man's shirt with different-colored paint all over it. Her hair is up in a messy bun. Lily can see a piano against the living room wall and an easel spread out facing the window.

"We want to see our dad," Annabelle says.

Lily hates to say it, but Fern's prettier than her mother. She's got slender arms and her toenails are painted purple.

"He'll be back in a bit," she says. "Make yourself comfortable. I'll get you something to drink."

Fern walks into the kitchen. Lily stays sitting on the couch, but Annabelle gets up and walks around. She picks up a wooden bowl that's sitting on the mantle.

"It's margarita mix without the booze," Fern says, handing them the drinks. "That's all I've got right now."

A dog runs through a dog door. Its leash drags on the ground behind him. Lily holds out her palm and he licks it. Annabelle notices Fern looking at the Band-Aids on her palms.

"This wasn't an accident," Annabelle says, peeling back the Band-Aid so Fern can get a closer look. "It was on purpose."

Fern's cell phone rings and she walks into the kitchen to answer it.

"Yes," Lily hears her say, "yes, they're here."

Lily and Annabelle sit on the curb and wait for their mom. Fern gave them plastic cups full of margarita mix to go. Jerry's truck drives up. Their mother gets out and gives them a big hug.

"What the hell were you thinking?" their mother says. "Running off like that?"

On the ride home, their mom sits next to Jerry in the cab. She touches his knee once, but he keeps staring straight ahead, his eyes on the road. Lily notices that one of his eyes is full of red veins, but that the other has none.

When they get to the apartment, their mother asks Jerry to come up, but he shakes his head no.

"Early shift tomorrow," he tells her.

"And that's that," their mom tells the girls as Jerry drives off. "Even the really nice ones have a breaking point."

But their mother's wrong. Jerry stops over the next night. He comes up the stairs carrying a new bathroom door. Annabelle's sitting at the kitchen table when he walks inside. Her walkie-talkie's broken and she's removed the casing to see if she can get it to work again.

"Can you fix it?" Annabelle asks Jerry.

Jerry goes out to his truck and returns with a tool kit with some very small screwdrivers. He works on the walkie-talkie for a few minutes, pulling on a few wires. Soon there's the cackle of static again.

"Time for bed," their mom tells them.

The girls fall asleep to the noise of Jerry's drill in the next room and the lonely sighs of truckers calling out for company. When they wake up the next morning they find the old bathroom door draped over their bodies, keeping them warm.

ALLIANCES

I bring a bag of balloons and a mini helium tank to the park. My dog Tater takes a crap by the basketball court and I pick it up with a baggie. I blow up a bouquet of balloons and tie the baggie onto them and then Tater and I sit on the park bench and watch everything float away.

As we sit there, a homeless man flops down next to us. He's wearing cutoff camouflage shorts and a T-shirt with the words "Cabo San Lucas" on it. There's a paper clip and some rice caught in the man's long beard. He's a bruiser, large biceps and big thighs. He's perfect.

"Excuse me," I say, "would you like to form an alliance?"

The man looks me over. I've just turned fifteen. I'm dressed like a skater, even though I don't skate. I've gotten sick of trying to grow a moustache, so I've just penciled one in.

"Is this some sort of dicksuck thing?" he asks. "Because I'm not down for anything dicksuck."

"It's the furthest possible thing from being dicksuck," I say. "The furthest possible thing."

The man pulls a bottle of whiskey from his backpack and takes a swig. He takes off his shoe and reconfigures his sock.

"Would this alliance get me some of that helium?" he asks me.

We're sitting near a water fountain that looks like a big dandelion. The fountain was recently shut down by the city because people kept getting caught having sex in it. I can see the fountain from the window of our apartment. I miss its soft lighting and the people who used to grope underneath its spray.

"You'd get all the helium you could ever want," I say.

The man runs his tongue over his chapped lips. He's not looking at me at all; he's staring right at my helium tank like I'm not even there.

"Then we've got a deal," he says.

I shake his hand and hand him the tank. He puts the release valve up to his mouth and inhales. I watch as his eyes roll back in his head.

"My name's Frankie," he says to me in a very high voice.

When I get back to my apartment, my sister, Ellen, is sitting at our dining room table. She's wearing sunglasses. She has a cardigan sweater draped over her shoulders. She's running her fingertips over my mother's old braille book, *Braille for a New Century*, moaning gently like my mother used to moan whenever she read braille.

"Are you still pretending to be blind?" I ask.

Ellen just turned twenty-two. She became my legal guardian two years ago, after my mom died. For a long time it was just Ellen and me and it was wonderful. Then she met her new boyfriend/acting coach, Cal, in an acting chatroom and a few days later he just showed up at our apartment with his suitcase. Now, through a variety of week-long method acting exercises, Cal is training Ellen to become a world-class actress. Last week Ellen pretended to be deaf. Before that she wore a hockey helmet and was mesmerized by jingling keys. The week before that, she wore an overcoat and talked with a British accent.

"Who's your new friend?" she asks me.

I see my binoculars on the kitchen counter and realize she's been spying on me.

"If you're blind, how did you see what I was doing in the park?" I ask.

Ellen's hands graze over the bumps in the braille book lightly, like she's playing a harp. She chuckles a little—like there's a joke her fingers just relayed to her brain.

"My other senses are heightened," she tells me. "That's what happens when you lose one of them. The other ones step up."

Ellen taps her way over to the refrigerator with my mom's old cane. She slides her hand inside the fridge and rummages around exactly like my mother used to rummage. She opens a jar of pickles, pulls one out, and takes a snapping bite.

"That guy in the park asked for directions," I say. "That's all it was."

Ellen makes her way out to the living room. On the way there, she smacks me in the shin with her cane. Hard. Her face shows no emotion. It's like she'd smacked a parked car or an ottoman.

"Sure," she tells me, "sure."

When Ellen goes to the grocery store, Tater and I turn on the TV and watch our favorite reality show. There's a very exciting race happening. To win the race you have to paddle a log boat out to a totem pole in the middle of a river and then you have to shimmy up the pole and grab a red flag. Whoever does this the fastest won't have to eat beetles for dinner.

While we're watching, Cal comes home. He takes off his coat and walks into the living room. He stands right in front of the TV, blocking our view.

"Didn't we already talk about this shit?" he asks.

Cal and I talked about this shit last week. He sat me on the couch and gave me a stern lecture about how reality television is killing legitimate acting, how television is killing legitimate theatre, how everyone only wants to watch dumbass people doing dumbass things and if I watch them doing these dumbass things, I am, by extension, a dumbass.

"I guess we're going to do this the hard way," Cal says.

I watch as he lifts up the television and carries it over to the window. He leans it on the ledge and pushes it out. I run to the window just in time to see it crash down on the parking lot below.

"Doesn't that feel better?" Cal asks me. "You're freed from your yoke."

After he says this he opens his arms like he wants to give me a hug, like he's trying to be my new dad. Instead of a hug, I take a swing at him. It's an awkward and telegraphed punch from a gangly, weak arm and he ducks it easily.

"Not a good idea," he says, putting up his fists and starting to circle me. "I've been taking stage fighting classes for years."

He circles me for a few seconds and then rifles a punch into my stomach. I buckle over, out of breath. Luckily, before he can get in another shot, Ellen comes home.

"Everything okay in here?" she asks.

"Just a little roughhousing," Cal tells her. "No big deal."

The next morning, Tater's sick. One minute he's eating his kibble and then the next minute he has a seizure. I carry him over to Ellen's bedroom and bang on her door.

"It's Tater," I yell.

The door swings opens and Cal stands in front of me in his underwear.

"Something wrong with your little doggie?" he asks.

I can tell from his voice that he's involved in this, that it's revenge for me taking a swing at him yesterday, that it's revenge for simply existing in my sister's life. I see Ellen behind him, lying on the bed in her bra and panties, wearing her sunglasses.

"Please help," I ask her.

Ellen gets up from the bed and slowly taps her way over to me. Tater's breath is shallow and then it stops.

"What's the matter?" she asks, like she can't see that his eyes are shut, like she can't see he's not breathing, like she can't see the black foam that's gurgling out of his mouth. I hold Tater's limp body up to Ellen's face like he's a sacrifice and she's some old-timey god who can snap her fingers and bring him back to life. There's a dead dog right under her nose, but Ellen does not step back, her nostrils don't flare.

"What's wrong?" she asks.

I wrap Tater in a fleece blanket and put him in a wicker basket and bring him to the park. I blow up a big bouquet of balloons and tie them onto the basket. I write him a note that says "I will miss you forever" and then I let him go.

Frankie makes his way over to me and we stand side by side as Tater floats away.

"That was a nice ceremony," he says. "He'll obviously be missed."

We watch Tater move south, toward the ocean. Frankie takes

a sip from his bottle of whiskey, then he hands it to me. I take a swallow.

"Where do you think he'll end up?" Frankie asks.

I tell him about the local elementary school that puts their school's phone number on a scrap of paper inside the balloons and lets them go. I tell him about how they get calls from faraway places, places you'd never imagine a simple balloon could get.

"They get calls from Peru," I explain to him. "From Russia. From Kenya. They get calls from everywhere."

When I get home, Ellen bangs on my bedroom door with her cane.

"Was your friend lost again?" she asks.

"Yes," I say. "But I gave him the directions he needed."

"I could smell the liquor all the way from here," she says. "It was like you two were sitting right next to me sipping on your bottle of hooch."

I want things to go back to how they were. I want Tater's warm body lying at my feet. I want to relax on the couch in my apartment with my sister while we watch our reality shows together, while we talk about how this or that strategy could work or backfire on someone, while we discuss how this person is a bastard or how that one is nice.

"I saw Cal with another woman," I tell her. "A blonde. I heard Cal call her 'honey' and saw him slap her ass."

After I say this, I see Ellen's eyes bulge a little, but she catches herself quickly, focuses them on a spot on the wall above my shoulder.

"You're lying," she says.

"Ask him," I say. "Just ask Cal and see what he says."

The next morning, I go to the party supply store and I purchase two large helium tanks and a bunch of balloons. I roll all of this stuff over to Frankie in the park.

"No helium until later," I tell him. "Okay?"

Frankie nods. I walk back to my apartment building and kneel down in the bushes by the front stairs. The window of our apartment is open and I can hear my sister yelling at Cal.

"He says he saw you with her," Ellen says. "He described her in detail."

"He's a liar," Cal tells her. "He's jealous of what we have. He wants you back and he wants me out of here."

"You're still seeing her, aren't you?" she asks. "You said you weren't but you just can't stop."

There's more yelling and then the door slams and Cal bursts out the front of our apartment building. I slide out of the bushes and walk up behind him with a two-by-four.

"Hey, Cal," I say.

Cal turns around to see who's calling out his name and before he can lift his arms to protect himself, I swing the board and nail him on the temple and he crumples to the sidewalk.

Frankie comes across the street with the wheelbarrow and we throw Cal inside and roll him over to the park.

"We're all set," Frankie says.

I see the hundreds and hundreds of balloons that Frankie has blown up.

"Is this going to work?" Frankie asks. "Is he too big?"

We tie balloon bouquet after balloon bouquet onto the wheelbarrow. For a while we think it's not going to work, that Cal's too heavy, but soon he lurches a couple of inches off the ground. We tie one more bunch of balloons onto the wheelbarrow and then Cal lifts off, climbing up into the air, over the trees.

I turn and look up at my apartment window. Ellen is standing there, looking down at us through her binoculars. I push the helium tank toward Frankie.

"Knock yourself out," I tell him.

Frankie puts the nozzle from the helium tank up to his mouth and inhales.

"Your turn," he tells me.

I wave him off, but he won't take no for an answer.

"All right," I say. "Just this once."

I take the nozzle from Frankie and put it up to my mouth. I take a deep breath in. I see Cal floating out over the city, higher and higher, heading out toward the ocean.

Soon Ellen runs out of our apartment building, not using the cane, not wearing her sunglasses. When she gets close, I call out to her. I yell out to my sister in a voice that is my own but that is also much higher and much more fierce.

ACKERMAN IS SELLING HIS SEX CHAIR FOR TEN BUCKS

It's a garage sale and Ackerman is selling his sex chair for ten bucks. It dangles from a beam in his garage. Underneath it there's a set of cross-country skis and a bread maker. The sex chair is brown leather. I check the tag—it's Swedish—very high quality. I inspect the various fucking holes—it's in great shape, very gently used.

"That's priced to sell," Ackerman yells to me.

I had a weekly thing with Ackerman's wife, Elaine, before she died. Every Tuesday night we met at a motel and screwed. She kept telling me she was going to leave Ackerman, but she never did. One Tuesday Elaine didn't show up at the motel and when I drove by her house a few days later I saw a hearse and a bunch of people dressed in black.

"What happened?" I asked one of the kids standing in her yard.

"Aunt Elaine crashed her car," he said.

There are a couple of other people roaming around in Ackerman's garage too. There's a young girl flipping through his record collection. There's an old guy rooting around in a box of tools. Ackerman's middle-aged, not much older than me. He's way too young to have lost a wife, but maybe too old and too sad to look for another one.

"That chair's gonna go quick," he says. "I wouldn't dillydally."

Ackerman's right. There's already another guy eyeing it. I look at this guy and can tell exactly what he's thinking. He's thinking about the chair's possibilities. He's thinking about where he could put it in his house, who he could talk into using it. He's not thinking what I'm thinking—how I miss Elaine so damn much that I stopped by her husband's garage sale to buy something she once sat in or touched or that still held the scent of her shampoo. Before this other guy pulls out his wallet, I pluck the price tag off the chair and hand Ackerman my money.

"Sold," he says.

Ackerman pulls the chair down from the rafters. Everyone else is gone now; it's just me and him. Grief isn't a contest, but suddenly I want it to be. I want someone to invent a grief-testing machine and then hook both of us up to it so I can show Ackerman I miss his wife way more than he does.

"You're really gonna enjoy this chair," he says.

What a normal person does now is says "thank you very much" and walks back to his car. This isn't what I do. Now that I'm here, I realize how badly I want to get inside Ackerman's house to see what other things of Elaine's I'm missing out on. The only way I can figure out how to do this is to pretend to faint. And so that's what I do. I roll my eyes back in my head and make my legs go slack and down I go.

"Oh shit," Ackerman says.

After I count to twenty, I open my eyes.

"Let's get you somewhere cool," Ackerman tells me.

"Yes," I say. "Let's."

I sit on Ackerman's couch and eat a banana. I assure him I'm fine, that this happens to me once in a while.

"Low blood sugar," I say.

He hands me a glass of water and I drink it down. Lately I've been listening to a lot of talk radio for company. I don't care what the topic is—sports or celebrity gossip or politics—I'm just really scared of it being quiet. I want to ask Ackerman what he does to fill up the silence, how he copes with Elaine being gone, but I can't let him know I'm anything other than a random garage sale pervert.

"Great house," I tell him.

I look out the window into his backyard. There's a garden bed with some sweet corn and cucumbers, there's a patio with a fire pit. Elaine always complained about Ackerman being selfish, not paying enough attention to her, but he seems nice enough to me.

"You want to see the rest of the place?" he asks.

The last time I shoplifted anything was in high school, but each room Ackerman and I walk through I shove something of Elaine's into my pocket—a five-by-seven black and white of her at the beach, a fridge magnet, a dart from the rec room. When Ackerman goes to take a piss, I slide into the bedroom and shove a pair of her panties into my pocket.

"I'm really sorry about all this," I tell him when he comes back.

"It happens," he says. "It's not your fault."

We're standing on his front porch now, staring out toward the street. A car slows down for a speed bump. It's a convertible, full of teenagers. When they go over the bump they bounce around, laugh their asses off. Ackerman stares at them and I see tears form in his eyes. I understand how something insignificant can suddenly overwhelm you, how any old thing can dredge up a memory that knocks the breath from your lungs.

"You want to grill up some burgers?" Ackerman asks.

"Sure," I say.

Ackerman fixes me a drink, tosses the meat on the grill. We sit on the back deck and watch the sun slide down below the horizon.

When Ackerman clears our plates, I run to the bathroom. I shove some fancy soaps and a hair brush of Elaine's into my pocket. While I am in there, I hear a glass shatter. Then another one. Then another. The shattering is spaced out enough that I can tell Ackerman hasn't had an accident, that he's doing this on purpose.

When I get out there, he's already got the broom out. He's sweeping the chards into the dust pan.

"You okay?" I ask.

"Just a little clumsy," he tells me.

When I leave, Ackerman follows me to my car. I move in a measured way, weighed down by all of Elaine's curios. While I'm loading the sex chair into my trunk, that pair of Elaine's panties I stole accidentally falls out of my jacket pocket and onto the ground. I quickly kick them under my car and turn back toward to Ackerman to see if he's noticed. His lips have pursed and his eyes are held in a squint. He's not looking at me, he's gazing up at the clouds in the night sky.

"We should do this again," he says.

"Definitely," I say, offering a handshake. Ackerman lets my hand hang out in the air for a long time, but then he finally grabs it.

"I'm a hugger," he says, and before I can stop him Ackerman pulls me into his body, surrounds me. I squirm a little at the beginning of his hug; wonder if he can feel everything else I've stolen from him pressing against his body, wonder if he can feel the picture of Elaine, or if maybe the dart is poking him in the thigh. He doesn't say anything so I settle in, get comfortable, hug him back. We stand there for a long time. I don't let go until he lets go.

THE INDOOR BABY

From his bed, my husband Mitch yells for fresh air and sunlight for our son. He argues that this is child abuse; that Swayze needs to be an indoor/outdoor baby, not just an indoor one.

"For the love of God, Mona," he tells me, "stop this now."

I empty out Mitch's catheter bag. I bring him his protein shakes. I flip his body to keep the bedsores at bay. While I care for him, Mitch never fails to remind me that he used to charge enemy bunkers and root around in mountain caves, always ready to meet his maker.

"Of all the crazy shit I've seen," he says, "what you're doing to Swayze is the shithouse craziest."

We live in an isolated area, in a rambler surrounded by a thick stand of Norway pine. Our winding driveway is washed out, treacherous even in daylight. Mitch's parents died years ago and the only visitors we get now are my mom and James, the delivery boy from the grocery store. I've tried to convince Mitch that Swayze's safer living like this, but Mitch won't be convinced.

"This isn't about his safety," he yells, "it's about your irrational fear."

Mitch was a ranter even before that landmine took his legs, but since then he's gotten much worse. I usually play the role of the good wife and let him scream and gnash his teeth all he wants, but sometimes when his rant gets especially lengthy or loud I open up the Bible of indoor baby rearing, *Nurture Against Nature*, by the noted Swiss pediatrician and agoraphobe, Dr. Gustav Halder, and I drown Mitch out.

"The sun does not keep your baby safe," I yell at him this morning after he won't stop grousing. "The night sky does not help raise your child. Clean, crisp air does nothing for your baby's well-being. Wide-open spaces do not thrust your kid on a path to become a productive member of society. You do not plant a seed in the ground and a little baby sprouts up. Your baby came from the womb—and as you know from previous chapters—the womb is the most indoorsy organ of all."

Tonight I feed Swayze in the rocking chair by his crib. He's a good eater. I put him up to my nipple and he goes to town. The doctor called him a miracle baby and I couldn't agree more. He shouldn't be here, but here he is.

It certainly wasn't easy. Mitch and I tried forever to have him. We emptied out our savings accounts to see the best specialists. I took Clomid after Clomid. Our sex life turned perfunctory, timed by tiny shifts in my body temperature and punctuated by me hurriedly pressing my thighs tight into my chest.

One day I had enough. I tossed the pills into the trash and shoved my basal thermometer into the junk drawer. I crumpled up the cocktail napkin on my nightstand where I'd charted when my eggs were going to drop. On my to-do list under "Clean window blinds!" I wrote the words "Adopt a cute child!" Mitch and I never actually got around to discussing adoption because shortly after I wrote this phrase down, his reserve unit was called up into action.

"You knew this could happen," he told me as he pulled his duffel bag from the crawl space and shook out the sand.

I touched the gray patch of hair on the side of Mitch's head that was shaped like a maple leaf. He pressed his lips against my neck. He slowly ground himself into my hips and I dug my fingernails into his shoulder blades and pulled him down onto our bed. For the first time in a long time I didn't care what my body temperature was or if my cervix was going to be receptive. For the first time in a long time it was unplanned and desperate. When we were finished we were lying on the floor of Mitch's closet near his clothes hamper. Somehow one of my hoop earrings had fallen out of my ear and clamped itself around his ankle.

"You've done your part for God and country," I told him as I untwisted my legs from his ass. "Can't it be someone else's turn?"

Mitch stood up and grabbed all of his underwear from his underwear drawer and dumped them into his suitcase. I'd fallen in love with Mitch because he had thoughtful eyes and a strong chin and because I fit into his chest when we danced, but I'd also fallen in love with him because he was a man who never shirked his duty. Now I realized that I was willing to love him a little less in one way to love him a little more in another.

"Honey," he told me. "It's everyone's turn. It's everybody's turn always."

When Mitch left, I missed hearing his gentle snoring fill our bedroom. I missed how his long fingers could always fix that crick in my neck. I missed the good chicken chili he made on Sunday nights.

A few weeks after he was gone, I went to the doctor to get a mole on my leg checked out. The mole had looked like a skinny

Ohio for my entire life but had suddenly morphed into a fatter Tennessee.

"That mole is nothing to worry about," the doctor told me, "but you're pregnant."

I was shocked. I called Mitch from the parking lot of the clinic, heard the clicking of phone interchanges from country to country as my call snaked its way to him over land and sea.

"You need to come home now," I told him. "There's no way in hell I can do this alone."

"You know I can't come home yet," he said.

"Maybe you could shoot off something nonessential from your body, like your pinkie, and they'd fly you back home for a few months to recuperate?" I asked. "Or maybe they would they send you home if you accidentally lopped off a decent-sized part of your ear?"

For my first trimester, there was no one to hold my long hair when I puked from morning sickness. There was no one to scare away the deer that kept traipsing through our backyard and eating our flowers and shrubs. There was no one to talk me out of going on the Internet and reading all the things that could go wrong with a baby inside the womb and everything that could go wrong with a baby when it was out in the real world.

A few months later I drove to the clinic and my ultrasound tech pressed a paddle against my belly. She said there was a boy swimming around in the sluice. Instead of giving my husband a hug, I had to give her one. Yes, Mitch continued to call me and yes, he reassured me things would be fine, but his phone calls were usually full of static or full of background explosions.

"Put the phone up to your stomach," he told me. "So I can talk to my boy."

I did this for Mitch during the second trimester, rested the receiver on my belly for Mitch to talk directly to our son. At the beginning of my third trimester, the baby began to kick the crap out of me whenever he heard Mitch's voice and instead of placing the phone on my stomach, I started to set it against my palm.

"Can you just come home for a couple of days when he's born?" I asked.

"I just told him I'd do my best to make that happen," Mitch said.

I wiped the phone sweat from my palm onto my pants.

"Of course you did," I told him.

My mother came to stay with me a few weeks before my due date. She'd just turned sixty-five, was fresh off her third divorce. Her latest marriage ended when she walked in on her husband, Dan, sucking on the back of her dog walker's knee. She thought her Pomeranian, Snowball, was partially responsible for Dan's infidelity and so she'd given Snowball to me.

"He could've alerted me to what was going on," my mother said. "It's as much that fluffy bastard's fault as anyone's."

I quickly tired of my mom's constant chatter about Dan and the dog walker and I certainly got sick of seeing her standing in her panties in front of my bedroom mirror, wondering if her knee joints still looked hot.

"Even if Mitch comes home in one piece," she told me, "he'll probably leave you in a few months because your hamstrings have gone all saggy."

My mother drove me to the hospital when my water broke. She held my hand and fed me ice chips during labor. We tried to update Mitch on my dilation, centimeter by centimeter, but his staff sergeant could not reach him. My mother called every half hour, but everyone told us he was unreachable.

"What does 'unreachable' mean?" she asked.

"It means that he's out on a mission," they said.

We called and called after Swayze was born, but Mitch was still on that mission. I knew there was something horribly wrong, but I tried to stay positive because I knew that staying positive would keep my breast milk positive and positive breast milk would give my baby a wonderful outlook on life instead of a dire one. Still, I couldn't help thinking that my milk was betraying me subconsciously, that it knew it was sad and worried milk coming from sad and worried tits and that it was probably poisoning my baby against the entire damn world.

After the second day without any word from Mitch, my mother and I began to escalate things, calling our senators and representatives, wading through governmental phone trees and their patriotic hold music and being stiff-armed by their secretaries and schedulers. Finally Mitch's colonel called back.

"I'm truly sorry," he told us, "but there's been an accident."

Each morning when I wake up, I like to read a random passage from *Nurture Against Nature*. Today I open to page forty-three and read this:

> *There will be some of your friends and family who will not understand your decision to rear your child exclusively indoors. They will not understand the logic. They will look at the light box you use to keep your baby from being seasonally depressed and they will shake their heads. It's unnatural, they will say, inhumane. They can certainly have their own opinions, but perhaps you should ask them why they do the things they do? Why are they submitting their children to the ills of carcinogenic sunlight or super viruses, why are they letting them get anywhere near unfamiliar pubes in public restrooms? How, in our crazy Amber Alert–colored world, can they let their children*

out of their sight for even one second? Listen to their answers and then ask yourself, are their explanations about how they raise their children any better than yours? Do their children seem any happier or smarter than yours do?

When I'm finished reading, Swayze starts to fuss. Swayze and I sleep in the master bedroom and Mitch's hospital bed is in the guest room. This is how it has been since the VA dropped Mitch off, gave me a live-in nurse for three days to train me on how to care for a man who couldn't use his arms and was missing his legs.

I set Swayze in his high chair and chew up some Cheerios for him. I put my mouth up to his mouth and spit the mush onto his tongue. I chew most of Swayze's solids for him because I want to make sure he will get the antibodies from my saliva and because it helps us to bond. Dr. Halder says that chewing up my baby's food will make him able to digest more easily and also make him less prone to dairy and nut allergies.

When I'm done feeding Swayze, Snowball runs inside through his dog door. I fill his dish with kibble. Next, I blend Mitch a protein shake and set it on his drinking tray. I prop a pillow under his head so he can watch television. I take care of everyone here, but there is no one to take care of me.

"Honey," Mitch says, "I wish I hadn't stepped on that landmine. I wish I'd stepped six inches to the left or six inches to the right. You shouldn't take out my bad luck on Swayze."

I position Mitch's straw on his lips and he takes a long swallow. I give him a sponge bath every day, but no matter how well I wash him or how many scented candles I burn there's always a tinge of urine underneath the vanilla or elderberry.

"Being at the wrong place at the wrong time isn't bad luck,"

I say, paraphrasing a line from Dr. Halder. "It's something you can help."

Later that day I call the grocery store for a delivery. James answers. He's the owner's son, home from college for the summer. He's got long brown hair that's always in his eyes. He's tall and lanky like Mitch used to be.

"How about two packages of diapers, a gallon of ice cream, a bag of pralines, and some chocolate sauce," I tell James.

"You making sundaes, Mrs. Roberts?" he asks.

"Uh-huh," I tell him, "I need a treat."

"We all need a treat every now and then, don't we?" James says.

"I need a treat more than most," I tell him.

"I hear you, Mrs. Roberts," he says.

While I wait for James to arrive, I bring Swayze to Mitch's bedside and set him in his Johnny Jump Up. Swayze hops up and down wildly, like he's trying to bust through the roof. I wipe away a thin line of drool that is extending from Mitch's mouth to his shoulder. I remember how I used to be hot for his mouth and it used to be hot for me. Even when we were in public, I used to feel myself curling my chest slightly toward it when he spoke, wanting its warmth and wetness. Now Mitch's lips are swollen, split in thirds like an ant's body, his teeth are always gnashing, snarling.

"How can you think this is a good way to raise a child?" he asks.

"Three hundred thousand copies sold worldwide," I say as I hold up *Nurture Against Nature* and point to a sticker on the cover. "You can't argue with sales like that."

Swayze keeps jumping, giggling maniacally. When Swayze and Mitch are next to each other, it's hard not to notice how much they look alike, the same almond-shaped eyes, the same bump on the bridge of their noses. When I look at Swayze, I honestly do not see one smidgen of me at all. It's like whatever genetic code of mine was mixed in to make him was gobbled right up by Mitch's genes. Like my genes were not the fittest of the bunch and they decided that instead of fighting they'd just lie down and get run over.

James's Jeep pulls into the driveway and he hops out. He's wearing a red polo shirt and khaki cargo shorts. He presses the button on the intercom.

"Hi, James," I say.

"Hello, Mrs. Roberts," he says. "I've got everything you need."

From our phone calls and our chats over the intercom, I know James wants to be a pharmacist, just like his dad. The last time we talked he told me that he'd just broken up with his high school sweetheart and he was taking it pretty hard.

"Come on in," I say.

James knows the protocol—I open the garage and he walks inside and sets the grocery bags down. Then he walks back out to his car. I press the garage door opener and the door creaks shut.

I watch through the window as James climbs back in his Jeep. His radio is blaring. It is a song with a lot of bass that rattles the glass in my hutch. He gives me a hang loose sign with his fingers and then drives away. Sometimes I wonder if he wants to know what I look like, if he thinks that someone threw acid on my face or I was disfigured in a fire. Sometimes I want to invite James inside and talk to him face-to-face, prove that I'm normal. Sometimes I want to let him see that I've lost all my baby weight, that I still look damn good.

In the garage, James's cologne lingers. It smells like rain with some citrus notes mixed in. I close my eyes and hug the grocery bag until his scent slides away. When I put the groceries away, I notice he's given me an extra bag of pralines, free of charge.

The next day my mother brings medical supplies and our mail. She makes the trip twice a week here now, on Tuesdays and Fridays. She's been very supportive of me; she doesn't judge our indoor lifestyle, she sees the advantages.

"You turned out the way you did because of the things I did," she tells me. "So who would I be to criticize? I'd be criticizing myself."

I put Swayze in his playpen and my mom and I split a ham sandwich. She tells me she's met a man named Jerome on the Internet. Jerome lives in Fort Lauderdale and she might go visit him soon.

"Jerome thinks my legs are beautiful," my mother says. "So thus far we're a perfect match."

My mother tells me more about Jerome, how he owns a catamaran, how he lives in a gated community, how he always wanted to have kids but somehow never got around to it.

"This may be my last real chance at love," she says, which is the same exact thing she said to me right after she met her last two husbands.

While we're eating, I hear a scream in the backyard. I look out the window and see an eagle trying to lift Snowball off the ground. Have you ever heard a dog scream? I hadn't. It sounds way more human than you'd think. I grab Swayze and all three of us watch as the eagle tries to get his claws into Snowball. Snowball bites and growls, giving the bird a good fight, but the eagle finally grabs him and flies off.

"What the hell is going on?" Mitch yells out from the other room.

My mother and I watch Snowball being carried away across the sky. This small white puff being pulled right up into the clouds and disappearing from our lives forever.

Today when I wake up I read this passage:

Your indoor baby will sometimes stare longingly out the window at the world. This is normal. Your baby is an inquisitive baby and he or she will wonder what is going on out there. Totally normal. This is how your baby tests their boundaries. Sometimes your indoor baby will bang his or her head on the window. Again, testing their boundaries. Sometimes your child will paw the window with their hand, run it down the entire length of the pane leaving these smeared and seemingly desperate handprints. All absolutely normal.

Swayze's first birthday is coming up. He just started walking. This afternoon he tries to climb up on the kitchen counter. Over and over, he keeps trying to hoist himself up, he won't quit.

"You are not going to be able to hold him for long," Mitch told me yesterday. "That's the thing. You think you'll be able to hold him inside here, but sooner or later he'll escape."

Mitch might be right. I haven't figured out how I'm going to explain all of this to Swayze yet. My mother thinks I should make up some elaborate story about the apocalypse, about a nuclear event, about how his skin will melt off if he steps outside. Luckily I've got a little while to decide.

After Swayze and Mitch fall asleep, I call the grocery store. It's only Thursday, but James has already been here three times this week. I don't know what it is with me lately, but I've become absentminded. No matter how many times I call James I always forget something I really need.

Tonight I order a pound of coffee, a bag of frozen chicken strips, two cucumbers, a bag of oranges, and a case of Diet Coke with lime.

"On my way," James says.

This time when James sets the groceries down in the garage, I accidentally close the garage door too quickly and he's stuck inside.

"Hello?" he calls out.

I immediately realize my mistake, but instead of opening the door, I press my ear against the door to the garage.

"Mrs. Roberts?" he yells out. "Are you there?"

The door's locked, but I swear I can smell his cologne seeping through it. For a second I think about flipping the deadbolt open, inviting him inside, but instead I press the garage door opener.

"You can let me see you," he tells me before he walks out of the garage. "I'd be all right with whatever happened."

This morning, on page 204:

> *Babies are hard work. Especially indoor babies. May we suggest that you buy a harness and stake your baby to something immovable? Don't skimp on the harness, because babies are very strong. Stronger than you might think. A baby with enough motivation can move a couch or a recliner or an antique armoire out from in front of a bedroom door. A baby with enough motivation can pull an oven off the wall and tunnel through the drywall behind it. A tip: when you do pound in your stake for your harness, pound the stake deep into the floor joists, so not even an adult can pull it out.*

Today when I am giving Mitch his sponge bath, I lean in to lift him up to clean his back. My shoulder is right near his mouth. Mitch could sweetly kiss me, but he doesn't. He tries to bite me. I pull away just in time.

"What the hell was that for?" I yell.

"We do our best with what little we have," Mitch tells me, then he starts laughing.

I don't understand what the hell he is talking about or why he's laughing, but I back away from him. I turn to look at Swayze . . . he's not there. I run through the house and cannot find him. Then I hear some squawking in the backyard. I look out the window and see Swayze standing on the patio and two eagles circling around him. He was just in his playpen a minute ago, but he must've escaped out the dog door while Mitch was distracting me. Swayze's wearing overalls and by the time I get outside the eagles have looped their claws around his shoulder straps. They pull him upward, trying to gain lift-off. Fortunately Swayze's a solid kid, much heavier than Snowball, and the birds only pull him a few inches off the ground before they set him back down and try again.

"Fight!" I yell to Swayze as I grab a broom. "Fight!"

But Swayze isn't fighting. He's jumping up and down as the birds flap their wings; he's trying to help them get off the ground. His jumping becomes more frantic when he sees me running toward him. I poke one of eagles in the gut with the broom handle and I knock the other one in the side of the head and they let go and flap away. Swayze is sitting on the ground now, holding out his hands to them as he watches them go.

Sometimes even with the best planning your indoor baby does not remain inside. Something goes badly. This is a time where you need to roll with the punches. Have a positive attitude, know which battles to fight, learn from your mistakes, have a steady hand, all of these things are necessary with any good parenting strategy. Your baby may not understand why these rules are necessary now, but later, later your baby will thank you for keeping him or her safe. Later, and this could be many, many years down the line, your baby will take your hand and look into your eyes and tell you all the good that you have done for him or her. Then all this hard work will be worth it, won't it?

I stand over Swayze now and watch his little stomach rise up and down. I gave Mitch a pain pill about an hour ago. He's snoring in the other room.

First I take a piece of plywood and I nail the dog door shut, then I pour myself a glass of wine. I sit on the couch underneath the skylight and watch the clouds move across the night sky. It's been a stormy summer and sometimes the wind blows so hard that I think the whole damn house is going to fall down around me. Mitch used to tell me that I was crazy, that this house was as solid as they come, but I still can't stop thinking that it just might happen, that one of the construction workers missed a nail somewhere, that maybe the trusses are moving in the opposite way the foundation is settling. Everything in the universe was mashed together all nice and tight at one time and then somehow it all blew apart, didn't it? Who's to say that the opposite can't happen and that at some point we'll all be smashed together again, noses into armpits and knees into crotches?

I pour another glass of wine and then I call the grocery store.

"I need a bag of marshmallows and a jar of peanut butter," I tell James. "I need a bottle of tonic water.

"Give me twenty minutes," James says.

I hang up the phone and then I go and check on Mitch and Swayze. I brush Mitch's hair from his eyes. Swayze's thrown his blankets aside and I cover him back up. When I'm finished, I walk into the garage. I press the opener and watch the door slide up. The wind moves through the tops of the pine trees and some crows flutter off into the dark sky. I unbutton my shirt, slide off my shorts. I throw my bra aside and step out of my panties. I stand there naked, waiting for James to bump up the driveway. I stand there, waiting for the lights of his car to wash over my pale body. I wait for him to see that even though I'm trapped inside, I'm still free.

FIELDWORK

Lessig's hut was closest to the latrine, downwind from the yucca being fermented in the hollowed-out rubber trees. He was lying in his hammock, itching a rash on his calf and wondering if tonight was the night the Kula were going to come through the jungle with their machetes and garrote his white ass. Three days ago, they'd abducted Tunney, who'd disappeared exactly like Rautins had the week before, without screams or hubbub, his hiking boots set neatly in front of his hut filled with stones from the river. Lessig and Schneider were the only anthropologists in the village now. After the first abduction, Gtal, the chieftain of the Campas, had ordered extra sentries in the watchtower and more warriors on foot patrol, but the increased security hadn't done dick, the Kula had poached another one of his colleagues. Even though he was less than forty-eight hours away from the supply plane splashing down in the river to ferry him away from this godforsaken place, Lessig knew he was probably fucked.

Through his window, Lessig saw candlelight in Mada's hut. He buttoned up his shirt as he walked across the plaza. He knocked on Mada's door and she grunted for him to enter. Lessig found her sitting cross-legged on the ground, weaving one of those shapeless ponchos he was so goddamn sick of all the women in Los Roques wearing.

"Where the hell have you been?" he asked her in his broken Utu.

"Around," she said.

"Around where?"

"Around around," she sighed.

Mada's hut was claustrophobic, one side of it packed with animals whittled from driftwood, the other crowded with baskets of dried fruit. Her bed was like a little girl's, the surface of it packed with braided palm frond dolls and throw pillows filled with quinoa. She was not particularly pretty, her nose had been broken and never reset, but she had a body that reminded him of a wasp, a skinny torso above a bulbous ass. A month after Lessig arrived in the village, Mada had gotten him drunk on something that tasted like kerosene and she'd pulled him back to her hut and unbuckled his belt with her teeth. Lessig was thirty-seven, newly divorced, his wife, Carol, stolen away from him by a classic rock deejay. After his divorce, he'd taken a leave from the University of Maryland to do some fieldwork and lick his wounds. He'd come to the rainforest to reconfirm his faith in anthropology, to make sure that his life thus far hadn't been an utter waste, but when Mada yanked his cock from his cargo pants he could not have cared less about any of that crap. Her mouth was wet and a little gritty and he busted his nut instantly, like a schoolboy, Mada pulling away right before he shot his skeet onto the thatched wall of her hut. Lessig tried to laugh it off, but Mada clucked her tongue in disapproval. She stood up and walked to the door, holding it open until Lessig understood that he should pull up his pants and leave.

In the weeks since, Mada had ignored him. And while Lessig should've been pleased that she wasn't spreading the news of their drunken liaison to any of the tribal elders or to any of the other anthropologists, Mada's lack of interest in him made his self-doubt blossom. If I could just talk to her, he thought, explain to her that he hadn't been touched in over a year; explain to her that his performance that night wasn't indicative of his overall sexual skill set. A couple of days ago, Lessig followed Mada into the jungle, hoping to set the record straight, but she saw him trailing her and lost him by the caves near the waterfall. Now that she was back she wouldn't even make eye contact.

"I was worried about you," Lessig said. "I thought you'd gotten snatched up too."

"I had to work out some things," she told him.

"What things?" he asked.

Mada sucked in air through her teeth. She dug her heels into her cocoa shell floor until she hit the hard clay beneath.

"Things things," she grunted.

Mada got up, took a guava from her table and broke it open with her splitting stone. She ate without offering Lessig any. She was a brusque woman, childless, widowed at an early age. During a communal dinner a few weeks ago, Lessig had seen her slap a boy who'd eaten more than his fair share of rice. After she'd finished with the boy, she'd lectured the boy's mother for her lack of oversight.

"Everything's bad now," Lessig told her. "Tunney and Rautins are probably dead and Schneider and I are next."

Mada took out a clay frog necklace from a basket, tossed it to Lessig.

"Wear this and you'll be safe," she told him.

Lessig still wanted to talk, but Mada was finished. She turned her back to him, returned to weaving her dumbass poncho. Lessig stormed out, slamming the rickety door behind him.

For his postdoc fieldwork, Lessig had lived in the forests of Papua, growing a gnarly beard and contracting malaria. He returned stateside with rock-hard abs and a sense of purpose, but the last ten years of lecturing in low-slung campus buildings and eating salt-and-vinegar-flavored potato chips had beaten down his vigor. Lessig's return to the rainforest was a chance to reclaim the enthusiasm he'd lost, but after only a few days of the bugs and heat, he realized he'd made a huge mistake, that he didn't want to live this hard life any more than his Anthropology 101 students wanted to listen to him prattle on about its beauty and simplicity.

After Carol had left him, Lessig moved in with his alcoholic father, a retired real estate agent who liked to have his television on all hours of the day and night. While he was living there, Lessig became addicted to the Home and Garden Channel, especially to a show called *Curb Appeal.* Most nights he sat on the couch gulping wine with his father and his father's alcoholic girlfriend, Dottie, the three of them watching designers tweak house after house to make them more salable.

"Lipstick on a pig," Dottie would say whenever the designers were stuck with a dud. "Like bright red lipstick on a Botox-lipped pig."

Sometimes on his way home from work, Lessig drove past his old condo, where Carol still lived. If the weather was decent, he'd park his car and crouch down in the bushes to look in her windows. One night Carol saw him hunched outside and called the cops. Lessig had been slapped with a trespassing charge and then a restraining order.

"When a wife leaves you," Lessig's father explained after he bailed him out, "you find another one. Maybe she drinks more than your last wife. Maybe she's not as smart. Maybe you realize you made another mistake. Whatever the case is, you make peace with it and trudge forward."

When he got back to his hut, Lessig strung the clay frog around his neck and put on a pot for tea. Recent rains had made the river majestic, full of whirling currents. Everyone else in Los Roques had a great view of the water, but Lessig's hut was behind a thick stand of palms and he could only see a sliver of it. He dropped a bag of Earl Grey into his cup and listened to the macaws bicker. It was midnight, shouldn't they be asleep? They were not asleep. They were alive and unbidden like everything else here.

Lessig readied his mosquito netting and wet some Kleenex to stuff into his ears to stifle the sounds of the jungle. This was the one point in his day he savored. A moment of peace in this shitty existence he'd led for the past few months. A moment when he could block out everything foul, when he could shut his eyes and dream of convenience, of hot water gushing out of a shiny tap, of his mouth being safe from stink bugs. He'd only filled one of his ears with Kleenex when Schneider pounded on his door.

"Any word on Tunney and Rautins?" Schneider asked.

Schneider was blond and tall and twenty-six years old and his skin looked like it did not have any pores. Lessig was stocky and dark haired and had stopped applying sunblock in the last few days in the hopes that a better tan might help him blend in with the natives when the Kula showed up again.

"The search party got back a little while ago," Lessig said. "They didn't find anything."

Lessig had tried to hate Schneider but could not. Schneider kept a knife strapped to his belt and had once saved Lessig's life by scaring away a jaguar that lunged at them while they gathered firewood. He also had a large cache of liquor and weed he readily shared. While Schneider was generally clueless about what it meant to be an anthropologist, Lessig knew he probably wasn't doing the Campas a huge disservice by acting like a bemused tourist, constantly snapping pictures, overdocumenting everything that happened in the village.

"Totally fucked," Schneider said. "One day they're here and then the next they're gone. Into the goddamn gorilla's mist."

Schneider had bunked in Lessig's hut for a week when they'd first arrived. He'd just finished a postdoc at Georgia Southern, which he kept referring to as "a party school." He brought presents for Gtal, a Georgia Southern hoodie and an expensive pen set, and after he presented his gifts to the chief, Schneider was immediately invited to live in a better hut, one with a wonderful view of the river, one with a female servant, Yelma, who sometimes cleaned his hut topless.

All of them had contaminated the tribe, Lessig knew, all of these anthropologists, coming year after year to study the Campas' innocence, even though they all knew that studying innocence was the one thing that always ruined it. When Lessig's department chair suggested he do his sabbatical in Los Roques to recharge his batteries, he talked about a world where traditions were passed down like heirlooms, people doing the same exact things in the same exact way their ancestors had a thousand years ago—sharpening rocks into spear tips, binding thatch to keep out monsoon rain, catching tarpon in woven baskets—and while all those things ended up being real, Gtal was also parading around in an oversized Georgia Southern hoodie.

"They were cutting apart a parrot outside Htul's hut a few minutes ago," Schneider told him. "Some fertility thing to help Htul's wife conceive. Lots of blood."

Schneider held up his Nikon to Lessig, scrolled through the pictures of the blue and yellow bird, first with two wings, then one, then none, then its head lopped off and bleeding out in the white sand. The last picture was a grinning selfie of Schneider's face inches away from the bird's head.

"Two more days," Schneider yelled back to Lessig as walked away. "Two more days and then that plane splashes down, brother."

The next morning, Lessig woke to find a pile of dead fish stacked like a teepee outside his door. Inside the fish teepee were his spare hiking boots, filled with what looked to be butter. Schneider came over to look, circling around the fish teepee with his camera, snapping pictures. Lessig kicked the pile of fish over so he would stop.

"I'm trying not to freak out here," Lessig yelled at Schneider. "I'm trying not to freak out even though there are fish stacked outside my hut like a fucking teepee and my boots are filled with some sort of butter or butter substitute."

"You've got to stay calm," Schneider said. "We're stuck. We wouldn't stand a chance out in the forest alone."

Lessig knew that Schneider was right. It was a four-day walk to a passable road through Kula-controlled forest in blinding heat. They could die any number of ways—caught in a foot trap, withered by dehydration, bitten by a deadly spider, buried in a mudslide.

"Do you want to watch Yelma clean my place?" Schneider asked him. "It always helps calm me down."

Lessig picked up one of the dead fish and hurled it like a discus into the river. He scooped some of the butter out of his boot with his fingers and flicked it onto the ground.

"You got any of that weed left?" he asked Schneider.

Later that afternoon, Lessig and Schneider were wasted out of their gourds. They were watering the garden plot when the search party came back from the jungle. Schneider and Lessig walked over to the group and watched as Bartik dumped Rautins's head and Tunney's hand out from his satchel. Rautins's head had been shrunken to the size of a cantaloupe. Tunney's hand was the opposite—it looked like a catcher's mitt, swollen to five times its normal size. Rautins's mouth was held in a scream, his eyes full of fear. Tunney's wedding band was still around his ring finger, cinching it like a twist tie.

"That's a head?" Lessig yelled at Bartik. "That's a hand?"

Bartik nodded, showing no emotion. It was all the same to Bartik. Huge hands, tiny heads. Just another day in the jungle.

Schneider pulled Lessig back to his hut. "We're gonna make it," Schneider told him, stuffing his one hitter and putting it into Lessig's palm.

"Sure we are," Lessig said as he inhaled.

That night was windless and Lessig stared out his window, tracking any strange sounds or weird movements in the brush. There was a bonfire down on the beach tonight, the night patrol chucking log after log into the fire pit until the blaze touched the sky. Across the plaza, Lessig saw there was candlelight in Mada's hut. He knew he should stay put, but he finger-combed his hair and grabbed the spear Htul had given him for protection. He was about to knock on Mada's door when he heard giggling. Lessig knelt down, peered into inside through a small crack in the thatch door. He saw Mada lying naked in her hammock and Schneider sliding around the room, snapping picture after picture of her.

"You're a natural," Schneider cooed.

Schneider kept taking pictures, pausing occasionally to pose Mada in different positions or fluff her hair. Soon Mada got out of the hammock and pulled the camera from Schneider's hands and kissed him. Schneider wrapped his arms around Mada and licked her nipple and her moan echoed around her hut.

In the way they touched each other, Lessig could tell that this coupling wasn't new, that their desire was not concocted through alcohol or loneliness. He could tell they had touched each other before, a bunch. He gripped his spear tighter, thought about bursting into the hut and pushing it up to Schneider's throat, making the two of them explain how this had happened. Lessig watched Mada pull down Schneider's pants. She pushed him down on her floor and straddled him. While he stood there, a sharp puffing sound came from the trees and Lessig felt a sharp pain in his arm. When he looked down, he saw a blow dart sticking out of his shoulder. Before he could scream for help, his legs buckled under him and he fell face first into the sand.

When Lessig opened his eyes, it was morning. He was bound, his arms and legs hog-tied to a long pole. He was bouncing up a mountain trail being carried by two Kula warriors.

"Where are you taking me?" Lessig yelled, struggling against the ropes.

The two men stared forward, stone-faced. Off in the valley below, Lessig could see trees being felled by chainsaws, bulldozers scrapping the forest floor clean. He heard chanting up ahead and he was carried into a clearing. About a hundred warriors were kneeling down in front of a stone altar. There was an idol carved in the altar that looked like some strange combination of a parrot and a pig.

"Please," he pleaded. "I can get money. I can get you anything you want."

Lessig was held down and lashed to the altar. A priestess lit a bundle of palm leaves and circled around him, wafting the acrid smoke around his face. She mumbled as she pointed to the construction below, mumbled as she held her hands up to the sky in prayer.

The math wasn't hard for Lessig to do. He was being sacrificed to a god who would try to keep the bulldozers at bay, who would try to stop roads from being grated and paved, power lines being snaked from pole to pole.

"I can help stop them," Lessig screamed to the priestess as she walked back to her hut. "Me. Not your god."

Lessig strained against the ropes, bucked his body up and down. The warriors started to chant, pounding their spears on the ground.

"I can help you," he screamed as the Kula surrounded his body, his words echoing off the mountain top and then returning back to where he lay.

INSIDE WORK

There was a tiny man mowing my lawn. Mowing the lawn was my husband David's job and when he left I let it grow. David had been gone two months now and the grass was almost as high as the birdbath. At night, I sat on my porch and drank Mexican cough syrup and marked its progress. As I drank I imagined there were huge snakes inside that vast thicket—poisonous snakes writhing around in there with their poisonous snake babies. Now there was this little guy, cutting everything down.

"Did my husband send you?" I yelled.

The man was rail thin and about five feet tall. He wore a white tank top and black jeans. It looked like he had a teardrop tattoo below his left eye, but as I got closer to him I realized it was just a teardrop-shaped piece of dirt.

"Ma'am," he said. "I sent myself."

I watched him as he loaded the lawn mower into his truck. He was chewing on a red cocktail straw, really working it over.

I'd seen him around here before; he cut a few of my neighbor's lawns too.

"What's your name?" I asked.

"Ronnie," he said.

"Ronnie, you're positive no one named David Hallberg hired you for this?"

"Lady," he said. "I saw this mess and I cut it down. And now I'd like my twenty bucks."

I pretended to cough, and then to soothe my pretend cough I took a long swallow off my bottle of cough syrup. I was doing what any sane person would do in my circumstances—I was drinking large amounts of cherry-flavored cough syrup and interrogating anyone who crossed my path for any information they had about David.

"Did David pay you to keep quiet?" I asked. "Was that part of your deal?"

I was at least a head taller than Ronnie and much thicker in my upper body. I felt a sudden urge to pick him up and shake him until he told me the truth, but I'd done this to a couple of people over the past week and it hadn't worked out well. Instead, I handed him the picture of David that I kept in my wallet for occasions such as this.

"Is this the man?" I asked.

Ronnie studied the picture, pushed it back at me.

"Lady," he told me, "I don't know who this guy is."

After Ronnie left, I took a nap. When I woke, I scratched under my left boob and a ballpoint pen fell out. I lifted up my other tit to see if there was anything hidden under there and a cocktail napkin floated to the ground. I looked closer at the napkin. The phrase "A high tide lifts all boats!" was written on it. I immediately called my friend Liza.

"You don't know how that stuff got there?" she asked.

"I used to hide things under my tits for David," I told her. "He was into that. Maybe I put that stuff under there and forgot it was there. Or maybe David snuck in here last night and put it under there for me to find."

I remembered some of the gifts I'd hidden under my tits for David. One year, there was a gold watch. Another time, a bottle of cologne. Once on Cinco de Mayo, there was a chicken soft taco. The more I thought about the cocktail napkin now, the more it sounded like David. Maybe he was surprising me. Maybe he was announcing his return by hiding things in the cracks and crevasses of my body while I slept.

"Maybe you should cool it with the cough syrup," Liza said.

Liza was my best friend. She was recently divorced. Usually it didn't bother me that she couldn't see all the possibility and wonder I saw in the world. Lately though, I couldn't understand why she was not seeing the things I saw so clearly, all these signs that David was afoot.

"He's not coming back," she said. "You understand that, right?"

I remembered how David had slid out of our bed in the middle of the night, how he'd stuck a Post-it note to my forehead that said "Don't hold your breath." For the last few weeks I'd thought he was gone for good, but now there was this cocktail napkin. Now it was obvious to me that David was orchestrating his return. It made total sense.

"Oh," I told Liza. "He's definitely coming back."

A few days after he first cut my lawn, Ronnie returned to cut it again. He was in his tank top and black jeans again, pushing his mower across my yard. His truck was parked on the street in front of my house, the back of it filled with twigs and brush.

"You're on my route now," he told me.

He was so damn skinny—there were not many spots on his body to hide anything fun or important.

"What does that mean?" I asked.

"It means I come once or twice a week and clean up your yard," he said.

I didn't know if I wanted this service, but sometimes when I called Liza she didn't return my phone calls. She wasn't the only one—lately a number of my friends were doing the same thing. Maybe it would be nice to know there would be someone that kept tabs on me.

"Can I stop being on your route when David returns?" I asked.

"Sure," Ronnie said. "You just tell me when you want to stop being on my route and then I stop showing up."

The next day, I decided to get back in shape. First, I'd walk around the block. Then slowly, day by day, I would venture out farther and farther with greater and greater speed. Soon I'd do a 10K fun run. When David returned, he would find an improved version of me—a toned, energetic runner.

After a couple of minutes of walking around my neighborhood my tit began to itch. I reached into my sports bra to scratch it and found some Chex Mix in there. Under my other boob I found a scrap of paper that had the words "Never apologize for anything you like!" written on it. As I sat down on the curb and washed the Chex Mix down with some cough syrup, I looked at the note more closely. It looked way more like David's writing than mine.

"He's getting closer," I told Liza.

"He's the same distance he's always been," Liza said.

A few days later, I woke to the sound of a lawn mower and there was Ronnie again. I handed him his money.

"Do you do inside work?" I said.

There were a number of things in my house that had started to break since David had gone and I thought it would be nice to get them fixed before he returned.

"Inside work?" Ronnie asked.

"Like moving furniture. Like plumbing and painting. Inside work."

"Sure," he said.

"Then come back tomorrow at noon," I told him.

The first thing I had Ronnie do was fix my clogged kitchen sink. Then I had him paint the kitchen cabinets. While he painted, I collected all of the items that I'd found under my breasts so far and lined them up on top of my dining room table. I inspected everything very carefully, picked up each one of the notes and held them up to the light, hoping they would provide some clues for when David would return.

Later that afternoon, Ronnie ran out of paint and I gave him fifty dollars to go to the hardware store. I didn't expect him to return. I expected him to take the fifty dollars and disappear on me just like David had. I was mistaken about Ronnie though. He returned in a half hour. And besides the paint, he was holding a bouquet of wildflowers.

"This is to say thank you for hiring me to do all this extra work," he said. "I can really use the money right now."

I found a vase and set the flowers on my dining room table. As I watched Ronnie work, I had another idea. Maybe if David was watching me from somewhere nearby, maybe I could use Ronnie to make him jealous.

While Ronnie was painting, I snuck up behind him and slid my arms around his chest. When he spun toward me, I put my lips on his and slipped my tongue into his mouth. My eyes were trained on the front door while I kissed him. I was waiting for David to burst through into the house and throttle Ronnie for making out with his wife, but nothing happened. The only sound I heard was the keys on Ronnie's keychain jingling as he pulled away from me.

"That was very nice," he said, "but I probably better get back to work."

Ronnie was supposed to help clean out my basement the next day, but I didn't answer the door when he began to knock. That morning I'd found a note with the phrase "Taking care of yourself means telling yourself thank you!" underneath my right tit. There were also some M&M's and a Marlboro Light there. I had eaten the M&M's long ago, but had tucked the cigarette back under there for safekeeping.

"Your drunk self is trying to get a message to your sober self," Liza told me. "Can't you see that?"

I watched as Ronnie cupped his hands over the window to see inside. I sat on my couch in a spot where he could see me, but I kept my eyes shut, stayed perfectly still.

"Ma'am?" Ronnie yelled as he pounded on my door. "Are you all right?"

I watched as he walked back to his truck. I thought he'd given up, but then he walked around to the side of my house. My dining room window was open and he took out a pocket knife and cut the window screen. Then he hoisted himself up and slid his body through the window and into my house. He stood up and brushed himself off and walked over to me. When he got near, I opened my eyes.

"Are you okay?" he asked. "Do you need help?"

I did not answer him. I did not explain anything. I just took his hand and pulled his little body closer to mine. There was a nice breeze coming in through the open window and I pulled his shirt over his head and then I unbuckled his belt. I undressed him very slowly and very deliberately. He did not argue, he did not say a word. When we were both naked, I wrapped my body around his tiny body; I surrounded him with my arms and legs. I took this little man, I took him and I pressed him into the spots in my body where I hid myself from myself.

THE PISS TEST PLACE

My metal band Hymenoptera broke up so I got a job at a piss test place. They didn't piss test us to work there so during my lunch break I usually got high by the dumpster. One day, right after lunch, a girl named Julie walked in.

"I need to pass a drug test to get a job at the laser light show," she said.

I used to work at the laser light show, but I quit because I hated all the Pink Floyd and Zeppelin they played. Sometimes when I ran out of weed I still went there to get a contact high, but I always wore earplugs so I could get my contact high in peace.

"There's this thing about my test," Julie said. "I'm gonna fail because last night someone spiked my hard lemonade."

Since I started working here, I'd heard many tales of woe and roofied hard lemonades. It was difficult to tell who was telling the truth and who was lying. All I knew was I'd accidentally eaten some cocaine fudge at a party a few nights before and I knew how easily something like this could happen to a trusting soul.

"I was wondering," Julie said, pulling out two twenties from her bra and sliding them across the counter, "if you could piss for me."

Many people tried to bribe me since I started working here, but I hadn't taken any of their money because of my excellent scruples. In the last few days though, I'd heard some chatter about Hymenoptera reforming. If that happened I'd need some extra cash to unpawn my guitar and buy my amp back from my dealer.

"Okay," I told Julie. "Follow me."

Julie and I went into the employee bathroom. While I was summoning a stream I caught her peeking at my junk.

"It costs extra to see it," I said.

"How much extra?" she asked.

I hadn't charged anyone to see my junk in the last few months so I didn't know the going rate. I figured inflation had probably doubled what I'd charged last time.

"How about three bucks," I said.

"How about two?" Julie asked.

"You drive a hard bargain," I said.

Julie looked like a lady who might enjoy a longer striptease instead of just a quick peekaboo so I did an enticing, erotic jig, pulling down my boxers a little with each hip shake until my dick just sort of flopped out.

"I gave you the three-dollar performance anyway," I told her.

"I could tell," Julie said.

I'd worked up quite a sweat doing my dance and now Julie walked over to me and wiped the sweat from my brow with her shirtsleeve. Then she kissed me on the lips.

I'd had sex at work with Ellen, the office accountant, a few times, but Ellen was older and mostly she wanted me to say complimentary things about her ass in her husband's raspy voice, so sex with Julie was way more enjoyable.

When we were finished, I filled up Julie's piss cup and handed it to her.

"You're a lifesaver," she told me.

A few days later, Hymenoptera got back together. I lugged my guitar and amp over to our practice space. At first everyone was excited to see each other, but that excitement was short lived. After we started to play, our lead singer forgot the lyrics to one of our songs and the drummer threw his drumstick and nailed the singer in the back of the head.

"What the fuck?" the singer yelled.

"You need to take this shit seriously," the drummer said.

It took a while, but the bassist and I cooled the two of them down. We started practicing again. Midway through another song though, the singer quit singing and turned to face the drummer.

"I wasn't going to tell you this," he said, "but last week I boned Sadie."

Sadie was the drummer's girlfriend. He immediately jumped over his drum kit and began to choke the lead singer. The bassist and I started to load up our gear.

"That lasted way longer than I thought it would," he told me.

The next day when I finished with my shift at the piss test place, Julie was waiting for me in the parking lot. She had a big black dog with her.

"Your piss was bad," Julie said. "You cost me my job."

I figured she'd brought the dog along to attack me, so as they got closer I threaded my keys between my fingers in case I needed to stab the dog in its face.

"I'm really sorry," I said. "What can I do to make this right?"

Julie took the dog's leash and pressed it into my hand. "You can apologize to me by dog-sitting Rancho tonight."

I stood there while Rancho sniffed me up and down. When he got to my bag that held my weed, he started to bark.

"He used to be a drug-sniffing dog," Julie explained, "but he retired because he has seizures."

When he finished barking at my weed, Rancho had one of these seizures. He flopped onto his back and his legs started to shake. His dog eyes rolled back into his dog head. Soon all the shaking stopped and he popped up off the ground like nothing had happened.

"See?" Julie told me. "No big deal."

Soon Julie left and I walked back to my apartment with Rancho. Halfway there, Rancho started to bark at a garbage can. I rummaged around and found a Ziploc baggie with a joint inside. When I stopped by the frozen yogurt place, Rancho barked at my friend Carl, who had a handful of quaaludes in his pocket.

"That dog's a goldmine," Carl told me. "Take him to the laser light show and pretend you're a cop and confiscate everyone's drugs."

"Good idea," I said.

Soon Rancho and I were standing by the exit doors of the laser light show. Whenever Rancho barked at anyone I flipped out a fake police badge and told them to hand over their drugs. After ten minutes, I'd already scored two dime bags of weed and these really hairy-looking 'shrooms. While we waited for our next victim, Julie tapped me on the shoulder.

"This is how you dog-sit?" she asked.

I noticed Julie was wearing the uniform for the laser show, the white shirt, the red suspenders. She was wearing a nametag with her name on it. She'd gotten the job even with my bad piss.

"I thought you failed the test," I said, flicking her suspender.

"I let the manager show me his junk and I got the job," she explained.

While we stood there contemplating each other's lies and wondering which one had done the other person more harm, Rancho had one of his seizures. I quickly knelt down and stroked his cheek and held his paw until he came out of it. I guess Julie hadn't expected me to be such a competent dog-sitter or such a compassionate human being, because when I looked up at her she had tears in her eyes.

"This job is dumb," she said. "Let's get the hell out of here."

Before we left, Julie went and stole some money from the cash register and then she and Rancho and I bought some frozen pizzas. We ate those back at my place. For dessert we had some leftover cocaine fudge I had in my fridge. Julie and I ate the rest of the pan and then she and I went into my bedroom and I did my enticing, erotic jig for her again and then we had a marathon sex session and then we watched the sun come up while Rancho scratched his paws against the bedroom door and whined.

ATHENS, ATHENS

Vic's bulletproof vest is draped over the motel chair. It's thinly layered Kevlar, slate colored, perfect for the summer months. It has extra cargo pockets for ammo and energy drinks. It's awesome. I want to put it on and get shot in the chest over and over and never fucking die.

My bulletproof vest is puke green and doesn't have storage space. My ex-wife, Autumn, bought it at an army surplus store last Christmas, two months before she left me. The price tag is still on it—$299.00 plus tax. It feels bulky, which means it won't stop shit.

Vic sprays his vest with Lysol and pats it down with a hand towel. I don't clean mine, no matter how pitted-out or gin-soaked it gets.

"You can't get sweat out of Kevlar," Vic warns. "It burrows into the fibers and then you smell like beef jerky forever."

Vic and I are working in Athens, Georgia. We're in Greektown, which the locals refer to as Athens, Athens. We're subcontracting for the DEA, surveilling a smuggler named Santo Kristoff. We're doing the grunt work for the Feds, tapping phones and manning wires, staking out Kristoff in a Ford Econoline van with the words "Passmore Electrical" written on the side. We're the B squad, sent in to see if there's any glory the real agents might want to swoop in and steal.

Our employer, Kromberg Security Solutions, hasn't exactly rolled out the red carpet for this job. We're bunking in a shithole called the Acropolis Lodge. It's grasshopper season and the Acropolis is infested. They're hopping around everywhere, sliding around in the bathtub, entombed in the cubes we get from the ice machine. A couple of nights ago I woke up to find one of them bedding down in the warmth of my pubes.

At least the Acropolis has a pool. I go swimming a lot because I've found the pool is a good place to cry. I'm usually alone down there, but if anyone stops by while I'm bawling about Autumn, I dive underwater. When I come up for air I rub my eyes and say, "Damn they sure use a lot of chlorine in this motherfucker!"

Vic does some crunches on the carpet, then some knuckle push-ups. I flop down on the bed, unbuckle my belt. A grasshopper lands on my nightstand and I crush it under a coffee cup.

"You skimp on your house, you skimp on your car, you eat smack ramen every meal for the rest of your life," Vic lectures, "but you do not, under any circumstances, skimp on your body armor."

Vic's flat bellied. I've got the beginnings of a gut. It's already big enough that my bulletproof vest feels like a corset. I can't zip it over my belly unless I take a deep breath in.

When Vic steps into the shower, I scratch at the waistband of Autumn's panties that I'm wearing under my jeans. They're cotton, black and boring, not frilly or lacy. They're panties Autumn normally wore to the grocery store or to the doctor. They're comfortable and they breathe well. Before Autumn left,

I asked her for a pair to help remind me of her when I was out on the road. I should've realized something was deeply wrong with our relationship when she gave me these, but I didn't.

The grasshoppers throw their reedy bodies off the walls while Vic and I try to sleep. I've pleaded with corporate to move us to another hotel. I've held my phone out and let the accountants listen to the grasshoppers' constant chirping. Instead of moving us, corporate sends us earplugs, mosquito nets, two cans of Raid.

"Hope for a cold snap," Spiros, the manager of the Acropolis, says. "Pray there's a late frost that kills the bastards."

I don't blame Spiros. He's like us, he's not the owner, he's the help. He lives in a tiny room behind his office, sleeps on a pullout couch. He's going out of his mind too. A few days ago I saw him trying to chase the grasshoppers out of his room with a torch made from a magazine.

The pool is usually empty in the mornings, but today I find a girl curled up on one of the chaise lounges. She's young, early twenties. Her legs are covered up by a satin jacket from Ari's King of Clubs, the strip club down the street. When I dive into the pool, she opens her eyes.

"What time is it?" she asks.

"Too damn early," I say.

The girl has a wide mouth I want to be generous, but probably isn't. She slides off her cutoffs to reveal bikini bottoms and then she drops into the pool. She swims a few laps then hops out and towels herself off. I'm probably never going to see her again unless I say something to her right now.

"You just swam in my tears," I blurt out.

I can tell she's probably used to men blurting out strange things in her presence. She stares at me for a bit, gathers herself, her face slowly tightening into a smile.

"Sometimes I come here to rinse off the drunken stares of hundreds of horny men," she tells me before she grabs her stuff and hightails it to her car.

Our ops center is down the street from the Acropolis, in a renovated shoe factory. Whenever the air conditioning kicks on it smells like leather and glue. I complained about this to corporate, told them the chemical smell gives us migraines, makes us dizzy. Instead of finding us new office space, they sent us some pine-scented air fresheners and a box of Dramamine.

"Nothing new on the wire," Foot Nose yells out to Vic and I when we walk in. "Quiet as shit."

Foot Nose looks like a fetus; he can't grow a proper stakeout beard. The hair on his face is patchy, mostly coming in around his cheeks. He's been working overnights this week, twelve hours straight, fueled by Red Bull and Hot Cheetos. Right now his forehead is so oily I can almost see my reflection in it.

Grimace sits on a metal folding chair, puking into a garbage can. Grimace is pushing sixty, pear shaped, too old for this shit. Every time I walk by his computer, instead of clicking off porn, he clicks off pictures of beachfront time-shares.

"Take a sick day, vodka tits," Foot Nose yells over to him.

Grimace responds to him by puking again. His puke is green and leafy and it smells like when you stick a shovel into the wet ground and flip over the dirt underneath. He's told me if it was up to him, he would've retired long ago. It's not. He's dragging three divorces behind him. He's got a kid in college, one in diapers. He's going to be working until he's eighty.

While I type in my log data from yesterday's run sheets, I occasionally glance over at Grimace. He lies down on the floor, pulls his knees to his chest, moans.

"Retire already, you assface-looking mofo," Vic says, chucking a soda can at his head.

This morning Vic and I park the surveillance van outside Kristoff's warehouse. We've bugged his house, hacked his email, tapped his landline and his cell. The DEA keeps assuring us Kristoff's a huge player in the Southern drug trade, that he's smuggling guns up and down the Eastern Seaboard. Unfortunately for us most of his phone calls are with his wife, Lani. The DEA wants us to parse their words for code, but there's no code there. They're talking like a married couple talks. *We're out of toilet paper, we're out of milk. Can you pick up my blood pressure medicine at the pharmacy? Should we drive over to the mall this weekend and pick up that daybed we've been thinking about?* These are conversations I used to have with Autumn. There's no code here, the words only mean what they mean.

The headphones in the van reek of barbeque sauce. While I listen to Kristoff gab with his wife, I can't help but wonder what Autumn talks about with her new boyfriend, Randall. Randall's a personal trainer, so maybe the two of them talk about his rock-hard abs. Or maybe after they have tantric sex they discuss the aerobic benefits of tantric sex. Or maybe they talk about sweet things, like how many kids they're going to have or how goddamn long it took them to find each other and how sad and lonely they were before they met.

Before I left the motel this morning, I stuck Autumn's panties in my jacket pocket. I pull them out and wipe my brow with them, just to see if Vic notices. He doesn't notice the first couple of times, but the third time he catches me.

"Are those panties?" he asks.

"Huh?" I say. "What?"

"Lemme see those," Vic says.

I push them back into my jacket pocket, but Vic wrestles them out.

"Whose are these?" he asks.

"I stole them," I say.

"You stole them?"

"I stole them. Right out of the dryer at a laundromat."

Vic stretches them taut and then flicks them out the window onto Kristoff's lawn. I jump out of the van and scoop them up.

"What's the matter with you?" Vic asks. "You steal a pair of panties and that's the pair you steal?"

This morning Vic borrows a fan from Spiros. He unscrews the safety grate from the back of it. He sets the fan on high and flicks grasshoppers into it. My bulletproof vest is crumpled on the floor nearby, getting pelted with bug shreds.

"This can save your life," Vic says, picking it up and tossing it at me. "Have some fucking respect."

I brush it off. Out the window, I see the girl from the other morning sunning herself down by the pool. The last time I was here her hair was brown, but now it's dark red. I do fifty push-ups, put on my swimsuit, and head down there.

"Here for your morning cry?" she asks after I walk through the gate.

"You here to wash off your men?" I ask.

I swim a couple laps while she sits in the sun. Before she goes, she sets a card by the side of the pool. It's a coupon for Ari's, two bucks off a beer or a buck off a mixed drink.

"If you come to see me dance," she says, "then the next morning you could swim in both your tears and your glances."

I go into the bathroom at the ops center to wash the grease of my face. Grimace is in there already, standing in front of the mirror, pulling down the skin under his left eye. There's fresh puke in the garbage can. This round is black and sludgy.

"You ever gonna get that checked out?" I ask.

"What for?" Grimace says. "I've always had a weak stomach."

"That seems like more than a weak stomach," I say.

"If you knew me," Grimace tells me, "you'd know this is standard procedure."

I glance inside the garbage can. What came out of Grimace looks like something that should not come out of a human being. It looks like something that might spill out of a chassis.

"Abrodabo called again today," he tells me. "Sounded like he was calling from a golf course."

Abrodabo is our supervisor. He was hands-off for the first few weeks of our operation, but he's tightening the screws more lately, checking in hourly, pushing us hard to find dirt on Kristoff.

"What did you tell him?" I ask.

"I told him Kristoff's a pro," Grimace says. "I said we'd be lucky to get him for jaywalking."

Foot Nose and I partner up today. We drive to Kristoff's house and use the parabola mic to listen to him chat with his wife about her bunions.

"Are you going to get the surgery?" he asks.

"It's gonna hurt," she says. "And then there's the limping. I'll be limping around the whole summer. Who wants to be limping all summer?"

"You're limping now," Kristoff says. "Maybe this makes it better? Maybe after two months you don't limp anymore for the rest of your life."

When you get divorced you're supposed to be able to throw yourself into your work. You're supposed to be able to disappear into the long hours and forget what ails you. Unfortunately this job is too lonely, too introspective, too full of shitty fast food for me to do that at all.

"How much longer you think we're stuck here?" Foot Nose asks.

There are rumors that Kromberg's profits are down this quarter, scuttlebutt that our CEO just cashed in his stock options, chatter that the DEA won't be renewing our contract. Vic and Foot Nose are paranoid, sure that we're all about to get canned. Both of them are sending out feelers, but I can't summon that kind of energy yet.

"I miss my girlfriend," Foot Nose tells me. "I miss her titties."

He opens his wallet and shows me a picture of her. It's a grainy photo. She's naked in it, these big floppy tits hanging down nearly past her stomach. Her tits are secondary to the sadness I see in her eyes. I've been duped again, that's what she's thinking.

"What do you want from me here?" I ask.

"You say she's pretty," Foot Nose says. "And then I say thanks."

"Fine," I say. "She's a total knockout."

"Isn't she though?" Foot Nose says.

I rub the binocular calluses on my nose as I watch Kristoff massage his wife's shoulders. He and his wife have made it through the tricky parts of marriage, the years when there are options, when temptations can pop up from anywhere. Foot Nose pokes me in the ribs.

"What now?" I ask.

"When I fall in love," Foot Nose says, snatching the picture of his girlfriend out of my hand. "I stay in love."

I wake up choking on a grasshopper. It is midnight and I can't get back to sleep. Instead of going for a swim, I walk over to Ari's King of Clubs. I sit near the stage and drink whatever ten-dollar beer they set in front of me.

"Give it up for Eleanor," the DJ yells and the girl from the pool struts out on the stage. She's wearing a stars-and-stripes bikini. As she dances, her ponytail whips around. I set down a couple of bucks on the stage and she snatches them up. When her song ends, she sits down next to me.

"Eleanor's not a stripper name," I say.

"It's my real name," she tells me. "I make way more money than anyone with bullshit names like Chastity or Angel."

I see Grimace over at the bar, sitting alone. In this light, his skin looks green and his teeth look gray. The girls, even the real hustlers, aren't hounding him.

"You want a table dance?" she asks.

"Sure," I say.

Autumn had a lot of curves, was thick in the right spots, but Eleanor is a piece of balsa, thin and flexible, her ass about as big as both of my palms spread. She grinds on me and the pain in my back disappears.

"Another one?" Eleanor asks when the song ends.

I hand her another twenty, point over at Grimace.

"Give that guy over there one," I tell her.

I follow Kristoff alone today. He goes to the Asian buffet where he likes to eat lunch a couple of times a week. After the buffet, I follow him to the barbershop for his weekly haircut. Yesterday, Vic and I spent all afternoon watching him supervise the roofing crew that reshingled his house. I got a headache from the echo of the nail guns, had to lie down in the back of the van to sleep it off.

When I get back to the ops center, Grimace and Foot Nose are unhooking all our surveillance equipment, tossing everything into boxes.

"Corporate called," Vic says. "We're shuttered. DEA's sick of paying us for nothing."

I drink a beer while Vic and Foot Nose book flights home. I

drink a couple more while Grimace packs up his car. Everyone is leaving immediately, but I'm going to wait until morning. Foot Nose is on the phone with his girlfriend, whispering and giggling. I think about calling Autumn, but I know I'll need to get drunk first.

I want to see if they all want to grab a drink before we all split up, but I know to not even ask.

"Maybe our paths will cross again," Grimace says, shaking my hand.

After I go for a swim, I put on my bulletproof vest and Autumn's panties under my clothes. When I walk into Ari's, Eleanor is giving a fat guy a lap dance on a couch by the back wall. When she finishes, the fat man gives her a long, uncomfortable hug. I order a drink, down it, order another. Eleanor walks over to me.

"Is Eleanor actually your real name?" I ask her.

She goes behind the bar and gets her wallet, hands me her ID. It says "Eleanor Tricando" on it. "There's your proof."

While she's shoving her ID back into her wallet, a picture floats out of it, lands onto the floor. I pick it up. It's a picture of a little boy, with a wide smile, floppy brown hair.

"Yours?" I ask.

"Yep," she says.

She reaches for the picture, but I pull it away from her, hold it above my head.

"I should tell you he's cute, right?" I say.

She jumps up and down, slaps at my wrist. I'm only teasing, but her face turns hard.

"I don't care what the fuck you say about my kid," she says. She motions to the three bouncers by the door.

"You fucked with one of our ladies," the biggest one says. "That means your night is done."

The man's voice is weary, like he's been here since noon, like he just wants to head home to his family.

"Time to go," another one of the bouncers says.

The three of them start to push me outside, but I decide I'm not going anywhere, that I want to talk to Eleanor some more. They wrestle me to the ground, kneel on my back. I know I should cut my losses, go limp, let them chuck me out in the street. I don't go easy. My mouth is right next to the ankle of one of these guys and I bite him hard, dig my teeth into his skin until I hit bone. The guy screams and jumps off my back, but the other two bouncers start wailing on me, kicking and punching. My vest doesn't do shit to help. I feel every blow.

CANNONBALL

Lisa's father was shot from a cannon once. It was on *Circus of the Stars*. It's twenty years ago now, when her dad was playing Dr. Lance Turner on the soap opera *Sunset Beach*, but he still likes to watch his grainy videotape of it whenever he gets wasted.

In the video, her father wears a white jumpsuit and a silver helmet. He sheds his red cape as he climbs up the stepladder. He slides into the cannon, gives a thumbs up to the crowd. There's a long drum roll followed by a thunderous boom. Suddenly, bursting through the gray smoke, flying up into the night sky, is her father.

Usually when he watches this tape, Lisa gives him his space. Tonight though, she plops down on the arm of his recliner and watches his descent. She watches him overshoot the landing net and fly past the bales of safety hay. She sees his body slam down on the hard and unforgiving earth, sees him tumble head over heel, shattering his left shoulder, dislocating his right elbow, breaking both ankles and his hip.

"Maybe there's a movie on?" she says.

Her dad takes a swallow from his lowball while she slips on her jacket. He hits rewind.

"And maybe you should stop dating your weed dealer," he tells her.

Eric's her weed dealer and sort of boyfriend. Their date tonight is part work and part fun. A week ago Eric tore his Achilles playing beach volleyball and he asked her to drive his car out to the swamp to buy his weekly brick from his wholesaler.

"It's a two-hour drive," he tells her, "but it's scenic."

In exchange for chauffeuring him, Eric will pay her three hundred dollars. He's also promised to cook her dinner. He's the one who first called this a date, but Lisa is the one who keeps calling it that.

When she pulls up in front of his apartment building Eric hops over to her car. When she signed his cast last week it was totally blank, but when he gets into the passenger seat she sees that it has filled up and that her well wishes have disappeared underneath a drawing of a dragon torching up a blunt.

"You ready for an adventure?" he asks, holding up a bag of beef jerky.

She's trying to let Eric's enthusiasm for life work its charms on her. Instead of questioning his motives, she's letting things flow to wherever they're naturally going to flow. She's not obsessing over each word he says, she's not revealing all her needs and concerns too early on.

"Up for anything," she says.

They drive north. She doesn't leave Tampa much and she's forgotten what it's like in the swamp, every leaf and tree battling for its own sunlight, vines choking anything moored to solid ground.

She brought some Trivial Pursuit cards along to fill the silences. She memorized all the answers beforehand so she'll look smarter than she is.

"What president once sang 'Amazing Grace' with Willie Nelson?" he asks.

"Jimmy Carter," she answers.

"What Italian liqueur is made from bitter almonds?" he says.

"Amaretto?" she says, the lilt of a question in her voice.

After a couple more correct answers, Eric tells her to take a left turn. They bump down a dirt road.

"Over there," Eric says, pointing to a trailer perched on the edge of a pond. When they pull up the red rock driveway, the door of the trailer pops open. Eric's wholesaler, Terry, walks out, wearing a stretch-marked tank top that's so tight Lisa can see the darkness of his belly hair underneath. Three dogs, German Shepherds, their coats caked with mud, jump around him and bark.

"This your girl?" he yells out to Eric.

Even though it's vague, the mention of "your" and "girl" in the same sentence in regards to Eric makes Lisa blush.

"Uh-huh," Eric nods.

Terry frisks Eric first. Then he pats her down. His hands are strangely soft and he smells like oranges.

While the two men chat, Lisa wanders over near the pond. She kneels down and picks up a rock off the ground, hugs it to her chest. The sun went down two hours ago, but there's still some heat from the day held inside. Eric hands Terry a manila envelope and Terry hands him a duffel bag and then they get in her car and drive back to Tampa.

"Totally easy, right?" Eric says.

Eric tells her he is going to make her prawns for dinner but when they get back to his apartment he notices there are lights on his living room he didn't leave on. He gets twitchy, scanning the street for any strange cars. He sees he missed a call, checks his messages.

"Everything's okay," he says after he listens to it, "but I'm gonna need to take a rain check on dinner."

Lisa knows if she opens her mouth now, whatever comes out will sound needy or disappointed. Eric peels off three one-hundred-dollar bills from his wad, pushes them into her palm.

"Thanks for tonight," he smiles, kissing her cheek.

Lisa gets up the next morning and finds her father in his recliner moving his pencil around his crossword. He's not very good at them, but he read something about them staving off dementia so he gives it his best shot.

"What's an eight-letter word for pouring forth?" he asks.

They're close enough to the ocean to have the birds but not the fun. They're close enough to the beach that the birds carry things back from there to show them exactly what they're missing. A few days ago, a cormorant dropped a beach towel in their backyard. Last week, a seagull dropped half of a corndog on the patio. In the past six months, they've thrown away three deflated beach balls, two spatulas, a pink wig.

"How about 'effusive'?" she says.

Her dad arches his shoulders up for her to rub. When she doesn't do it right away, he clears his throat.

"Effusive works," he says. "So far."

He fills out the crossword like he fills out his days—cautious at the beginning, then with much more abandon. She often hears him rumbling around in the kitchen late at night. It sounds like shopping carts banging into each other, his cane smacking the stove, the refrigerator. She waits until all the noise has died away, when he's passed out in his recliner, and she carries him off to bed. He weighs next to nothing now, bends over her arms like a bolt of cloth.

"It's not a jaunt, it's a journey," he told her recently, "full of starts and stops to select our roles."

The roles they've settled on are these: He's the crotchety old soap opera star who feels the world has done him terribly wrong. Scared and broke, but unable to cop to it. She's the trapped daughter who drives off in her car with no intention of returning, but who always turns around before she reaches the state line.

His days are still full of frustration, jaw clenching, things that he cannot accomplish. The jar of pickles out of his reach. An imaginary mosquito always buzzing around his ankles. The way they communicate best is by him shaking the ice cubes in his empty gin glass and her filling it up.

After he finishes his crossword, they start his physical therapy. Lisa pulls and contorts his body into paperclip shapes. Each day she does this she finds he's stiffened, less pliable. She limbers him up with towels warmed in the microwave; treats his body as if it were day-old bread wet heat might soften.

"My slow trudge to sludge," he says in his gravely news voice. She presses him into a small package, his thighs up to his chest.

"Screw you," he grunts. "Screw you and yours."

"Right back at you," she says.

"You are killing me," he says. "Every damn day of every damn day."

They have their routines and the routines do what routines always do, take fear out the equation, tell your insides you're okay, make you able to corral your breath when your breath tries to run away.

"Just leave me to die," he says. "Put me on a burning raft and set me adrift on the ocean current."

"No money for a raft," she tells him.

"Then sell that body of yours," he says. "It's passable enough."

"It's a buyer's market," she responds. "You'd need more than I got."

They could go on like this all day, back and forth like they were in some black-and-white talkie, clipped speeches about just how hard it is to put one foot ahead of the other, how happiness is always slightly out of reach. Even though noir always calls for you to keep on walking until you disappear right off the edge of the screen, she stays put. She thinks it's sad to know the exact strength of every fiber of your body—your heart, your lungs, your legs.

A week later, Eric asks her on another date.

"Same deal as last time," he says. "Except this time the dinner actually happens, all right?"

Lisa picks him up and they drive through the swamp. Eric asks her some more trivia questions. *What state, full of milk and honey, was the destination in* The Grapes of Wrath*? What's the main vegetable in vichyssoise?* This time the ride seems shorter—maybe because she actually knows how far they're going. While she drives, Eric nods off. Halfway back home, Lisa sees a man standing in the middle of the road, flagging her down. At first she thinks his car has broken down, but there's no car anywhere around. When she gets closer she sees the moon hit the man's skin and she realizes he's naked. The man is weaving back and forth across the road, like he's drunk. She screeches to a stop.

"Shit," Eric yells, awake now, pulling a gun out of his jacket pocket. "What are you doing? Shit, shit, shit." Eric waves his gun around, looking for any movement in the brush, thinking this is a trap, thinking that dudes with machine guns will step out of the desert darkness and riddle their car with bullet after bullet.

Lisa stares at the naked man. He's about twenty-five feet

away from her, breathing heavily through his mouth. He's young with shoulder-length blond hair, clean shaven. She watches as he pulls a lighter from his palm and flicks it and his body goes up in flames. She sees the man crumple to his knees.

It takes her a second to register what has happened. She opens her door to get out and help him, to throw her jacket over his body, something, but before she can get out Eric reaches across her body and pulls the door shut.

"Drive," he tells her in a voice that seems much too calm.

Her father had a job a few months back, reading audio books, but he got fired. He has a perfect voice for reading anything—spy novels or travails of sappy love—all of the publishers tell him that, but lately he's too morose and stubborn.

"He'll get more work if he stops talking about death in between takes," his old agent Twyla told Lisa. "And if he stops being so damn pedantic. He's acting like he's Orson Welles or something."

His agent, Twyla, retired to St. Pete and she comes over to their condo every Tuesday night for dinner. She's going through menopause right now, full of hot flashes and gland puffiness. Twyla likes her dad, remembers the good times. After the accident, she could have dropped him as a client, but she stuck it out. She kept offering him up to casting agents, always hung up on them when they asked—*Who?* or *Isn't he dead?*

They're like an old couple, recasting themselves in stories long past—Twyla as the pretty young agent who talked like a sailor, her father as the up-and-comer who had a shot to be a leading man.

Sometimes Lisa wraps up little presents for her father to give to Twyla. Last week, her father gave Twyla a pair of earrings shaped like butterflies.

"What is in the box?" her father asked as he signed the card. "So I can pretend I know."

"Butterflies," she said.

Lisa didn't bother to clarify. She'd rather have him think there was something alive in there, that once the bow was loosed, something amazing might flutter out.

Lisa doesn't sleep much for the next few days. Every time she closes her eyes she sees the burning man, flopping and spinning around on the road. The morning after it happened, she drove back out to the swamp. She couldn't find a body, no burn marks on the tar, no evidence that anything actually happened.

"Did we break up?" she asks Eric after she finally gets a hold of him after a week of calling. "Do I need to find a new dealer?"

"You were a car," Eric tells her. "You were some fun for a day or two."

Lisa scours the newspaper for any information about the burning man. They run a missing person piece on a man named Christian Eccles who looks like the man she saw. He battled schizophrenia. His mother, Ingrid, was quoted in the story. She looked up Ingrid Eccles's address and called her. She told her she was a reporter, made an appointment to talk.

"I'm going to see his mother," she tells Eric.

"Let it go," he says. "He was crazy. You were in the wrong place at the wrong time."

"Will I ever see you again?" she asks.

"Sometimes the beauty of something is its utter convenience," Eric tells her.

Before she meets Christian Eccles's mother, she drives her father to have breakfast with Twyla. More than anything her father wants to get his license back. That's the thing he misses the most. He's gone down to the DMV and taken the test three times in the last year, but his hip always gives out on him halfway through the test and he has to quit.

Ingrid Eccles is a small woman, her brown hair pulled up in a misshapen bun. There are lots of doilies in her apartment, lots of pictures of Christian, a good layer of dust covering everything.

The pictures of Christian hang in chronological order on her living room wall, the naked youngster on the shag rug, the boy holding the baseball bat, the teenager with wings of hair feathered over his ears.

Ingrid can't sit still. She makes lemonade, puts out a plate of cookies.

"I can't believe he's gone," she tells Lisa.

As he ages, the pictures of Christian get fewer and fewer. In the last one, he looks off the rails, his mouth held in a sneer, his eyes watery and distant.

"They were having trouble figuring out his meds," Ingrid says when she notices Lisa looking at that picture. "At that point he hated any sort of camera being around him. Ever since he was fifteen there were signs. The drugs helped for a while, but then not so much."

Lisa holds a napkin underneath her cookie. She wants to ask Ingrid if she feels relieved he's gone, but she knows it's a horrible question. She eats her cookie, shakes Ingrid's hand, tells her thank you.

Later that week, Lisa is eating dinner with her dad at a seafood place near the wharf, a place with a signed picture of her father in a frame up on the wall. He's dressed up, she's not. They are an odd couple, her in paint-splattered chinos and a raggedy T-shirt, him in a slate-colored suit. The owner keeps coming over to their table, asking if everything is all right for "Mr. Turner."

"Twyla called me today. She heard they might resurrect my character on *Sunset Beach*," he tells her. "There's scuttlebutt. That's what she told me. Scuttlebutt. I would have been on a deserted island all these years. Shipwrecked or some shit. I come back pissed off and out for revenge."

When they get home, Lisa goes up to bed. Later that night, she gets up and finds her father asleep in front of the TV. His legs are propped up on a chaise lounge. His cannonball video is paused and he's frozen there on the screen. The picture is old and blurry and you can't really tell what is happening, so Lisa grabs the remote from off the coffee table and clicks forward a couple frames. That does it; it moves her father out of the haze. She sets the remote back down on the coffee table and leaves him sitting there, a man held in mid-flight, a man with no pinnacle and no nadir, a man unaware of the ground below.

CHET

My older brother Chet died after he got bit by a sick elk. It was a horrible death, lots of moaning and black puke and weeping styes all over his back and chest. Nothing, not any of the doctors at the hospital, not shitloads of morphine or the tenderness of the nursing staff, nothing could ease his pain. Poor Sick Chet. Poor Poor Sick Sick Chetty. That's what we all said.

Chet got bit on our annual hunting trip. The elk that bit him was one I'd shot but hadn't shot well enough. Chet got to it before me and he knelt down in the switch grass to field dress the beast. While he was unsheathing his hunting knife, the elk reared up and chomped down on his thigh, right through his Carhartts. The elk keeled over immediately after that, like that bite was his last wish.

At first, Chet shook off the pain. He gulped blackberry brandy and revenge-stabbed the elk in the face about fifty times—it was only on the drive home that he started to look green. I knew something was wrong with him when my dad asked us if we wanted to stop at the strip club in Lake City and Chet said he thought it might be best to skip the strippers and head straight home. I knew something was especially fucked when my dad and I dragged Chet inside the strip club anyway and he fainted before he even saw one goddamn tit.

Chet's newlywed wife, Flor, stood vigil by his hospital bed the entire time. Flor was Panamanian and she often wore her hair in pigtails and her dresses were embroidered with tiny flowers on the bodice and sleeves. She'd only been married to Chet for two months, but most nights she slept on a cot next to Chet's wasting body, feeding him popsicle chunks and dabbing his forehead with a damp washcloth as he drifted in and out of consciousness. Unfortunately, one morning she started to puke. It was regular yellow-brownish puke, not blackish puke like Chet's, but I was still worried for her. By then, I'd fallen under the spell of her dark eyes and loved the pragmatic way she stood by Chet's bedside as he fought his way though chill and fever, pain and fear.

"You're not sick," the doctors explained after they'd examined Flor. "You're pregnant."

Flor told Chet the news immediately, thinking this bit of wonder might provide him some sort of extra will to survive this horrible elk-biting disease.

"I'm with child," she explained. "Which is a beautiful thing, right? A baby!"

Chet was in a coma by then. He hadn't spoken in a week, but after Flor told him about the baby we heard him mumble, okay, okay, okay. We milled around his bed for a while after that, excited, hoping for more, hoping for a small signal he was still fighting. Unfortunately, those were the last words Chet ever spoke. A few minutes later his body seized up, every muscle in his arms and legs tightening and braiding, his torso bucking up and down on his bed. The doctors rushed in with a crash cart, but it was useless. Flor buried her head in my shoulder and sobbed.

"It was like he was waiting to hear about the baby before he said good-bye," I told her.

II

Five years might be a long time for some people to grieve, but it isn't for me. I still tear up every time I think of Chet. It's just how I'm wired. I end up thinking about Chet a lot because I can see his gravestone from the cafeteria of the power plant where I work. Sometimes I'll be eating a grilled cheese sandwich and I'll accidentally glance down at the graveyard and think about how Chet liked grilled cheese sandwiches and my eyes flood with tears. I can't help it.

A bunch of my other relatives are buried in that cemetery too. It's about two hundred yards from the power plant, overlooking the river. It's extra ominous because steam from the turbines billows over it and because there are always craggy old fishermen on the shore below, casting their lines into the murky bilge. It's great fishing if you like bottom feeders—suckers, carp, the occasional gooch that's taken a wrong turn from the gulf—all of them love the soupy water, all of them love being nearly boiled alive.

Today at lunch, I eat a chicken salad sandwich Flor has packed for me. My Uncle Jimmy, who also happens to be my boss, is staring out at the river with his binoculars. Jimmy is my mom's brother. Truth be told, this is kind of a family-run power plant. My Aunt Joan works in human resources, my dad was the plant maintenance coordinator until he retired last year. After Chet died, we got Flor a job in the childcare center, where she works with Uncle Jimmy's twin daughters, Elaine and Erica. Some people might call this nepotism, but we call it taking care of our own. And that's what we do, even when our own are total dumbasses like Allen, my first cousin, who works in the turbine control room and who, about two to three times per year, knocks out the entire power grid east of the Mississippi.

"Uh-oh," Uncle Jimmy says, passing me the binoculars.

I look down at the cemetery to see what he's uh-oh-ing. The old priest from town, Father Hollenbeck, is down there trying to dig up Chet's grave again.

"You've got to be fucking kidding me," I say.

It's the middle of August, 102 degrees. I was hoping to stay inside the air conditioning today. I was planning to take a restorative nap after playing some computer solitaire, but instead I holster my taser and tromp past the cooling towers and then over the catwalk that runs the length of the outtakes. I pass by Vince, Uncle Tommy's bastard son, in the guard shack.

"Didn't I tell you to radio me if Hollenbeck showed up again?" I ask.

"He said he was gonna put a hex on me," Vince says. "He held up his cross and muttered a bunch of Latin shit. I'd much rather just have you pissed at me than him."

When I get down to the cemetery, Hollenbeck's wiping his brow off on his vestments. The man's nearly eighty years old, but he's digging like he's twenty. He's already reached the top of Chet's casket. I see the gouges on the lid from the last time he did this.

"Sure is hot out, huh, padre?" I say.

Father Hollenbeck turns toward me, the sweat rolling down his forehead and catching in the folds of his face. He's getting worse. Last week, he walked into the produce aisle of the grocery store, pulled out his dick, and rubbed it all over the Bibb lettuce. I heard the church was moving him into assisted living, a place with large orderlies and locked doors, but he's obviously not there yet.

"Do I know you?" he asks.

"Bryce Jordahl," I say. "I was an altar boy a few years back?"

Father Hollenbeck pulls a flask from a secret pocket inside his cassock and takes a nip. He's forgotten to put in his dentures today and his lips look like they're being sucked into his mouth.

"I'd remember that," he says, "but I don't. Which means you've probably been sent here by the devil to confound me."

Hollenbeck clears away more dirt from around the coffin. His breath is gamey, full of scotch and garlic. I look at Chet's gravestone. It's not in the best of shape. There's bird shit streaked on it and someone keeps bringing flowers out here but never taking them away. There's a bale of decaying roses next to Chet's grave, curled together, smelling like sweet piss.

"Bryce?" I say, pointing to the name on the stone, "Chet's brother?"

"Whose brother?" Hollenbeck asks.

I notice a bunch of my relatives standing in front of the big windows of the cafeteria, my aunts and uncles, a handful of my cousins, all of them looking down at me. It is way too hot to pussyfoot around, so I grab Hollenbeck's shovel. Unfortunately, he sidesteps me before I can get a good grip on it and he swings the shovelhead and nails me in the shin. I fall onto the ground and writhe.

"God's will is God's will," Hollenbeck tells me.

While I rub my leg, Hollenbeck walks over to the casket. He sticks the shovel under the lid, rocks it back and forth, trying to pry it open. Before he does, I lurch to my feet. I unholster my taser and blast his ass, because priest or no priest, this mofo deserves to be tased. Hollenbeck yelps and his jaw clenches and his eyes bug out of his head and he tips to the ground. He's still breathing and everything, but he's just way less interested in digging up my dead brother now.

"Leave my family the hell alone," I whisper in Hollenbeck's ear as I slap the handcuffs on.

I stuff Hollenbeck into the cab of my truck. My relatives are all looking at me from the cafeteria window. Most of them think I've got anger management issues. Most of them think that just because I tased Allen after he stole my burrito from the employee fridge I'm a loose cannon. Most of them think I should've been suspended by Jimmy for much longer than a week for blasting my own cousin over something as insignificant as a burrito. I look up at all of them looking down at me with the judgey hazel-colored eyes that dominate my family tree, and I flip all of them off because guess what, fuck what the fuck they think.

Hollenbeck's still out of it when I pull up in front of the rectory. His eyes are open, but he hasn't said a word. I give his cheek a little slap but that doesn't help. His housekeeper, Ethel, comes out from the house and we carry him to bed. Once he's safely under the covers, he closes his eyes and starts to snore.

"He used to be such a peaceful man," Ethel tells me, "but he's the exact opposite now. He can't find any relief."

When I get home, Flor is in the backyard weeding around the tomato plants and I walk over and give her a kiss. Today's our first wedding anniversary. My dad is coming over in a few hours to babysit Antonio and the two of us are going to dinner to celebrate.

"The birds are back," she says.

Even though I call Antonio my stepson, since he's Chet's kid, he's my nephew too. For his birthday last year one of the presents I gave him said "Uncle Bryce" and the other one read "Dad." I look at him sitting in the shade of the big oak tree in our backyard. There are six crows sitting about ten feet away from him, their feathers pressed tightly against their bodies, their eyes unblinking, watching Antonio play with his Matchbox cars like he's giving them some sort of lecture.

"Did you stop shooing them away?" I ask Flor. "Didn't we decide we needed to keep doing that?"

For some reason Antonio attracts birds. It's one of the many weird things about the kid. Whenever he goes outside, the crows swoop down from their perches and park themselves a few feet from where he's playing. Antonio will hardly say a word to me, but often interacts with the crows, caws at them, whispers things to them under his breath.Flor hopes it's a phase, but this isn't any phase.

"Did we decide to start shooing again?" Flor asks. "I thought we were just letting them be."

I don't have the energy to shoo the crows away from Antonio so I just let them be. I just want to have fun tonight. Flor and I had to bargain with my father for the babysitting help. Even though Antonio's his only grandchild, the last time he babysat, Antonio told him he was going to die soon, that he was going to have a heart attack. Normally my dad would've just laughed a comment like that off, but at the grocery store a few weeks earlier Antonio told August Johnson he was going to drown. August tousled Antonio's hair and told Antonio that he sure had an active imagination, ha, ha, ha. The next night, on the way home from his dart league, August drove his truck off the Lester River Bridge and his truck sank and his lungs filled up with water.

"Hollenbeck came back again today," I tell Flor. "He almost got the casket open this time."

I skip the part about tasing Hollenbeck because after I tased Allen over that burrito, after he spent that day in that medically induced coma, after his life was sort of touch and go there for a few hours, me tasing anyone is a sensitive subject with Flor.

"That poor man," she says. "I wish there was some way to help him."

My father arrives and gives Antonio a halfhearted hug. My dad used to always bring along a little gift whenever he came to visit, a wood car or a Lego set, but tonight he comes over empty-handed. He sits across the room from Antonio.

"Be nice to Grandpa," Flor tells Antonio as we head out the door.

At dinner, I order steak and fries and Flor gets the pasta special. We quickly finish off a bottle of wine. It's so great to be out of the house on a date. It's been a while.

"I can't believe it's already been a year," I say, toasting Flor.

I'm trying to keep things upbeat, but truth be told the last year has been difficult. A few months ago I came home early from work and found Flor in our bed rubbing an eight-by-ten picture of Chet against the crotch of her jeans. I hadn't thought about it much before, but it really made me start to wonder—was she happier with Chet than she was with me? Was Chet a better husband? A better lover? It's hard to compete with a dead man because all of the jackass things he did that have been washed away by time and all the jackass things I do keep on happening every day.

"It flew by," she says.

On the way home, I swing by Beacon Point. As a surprise, I pull out a checkered tablecloth and spread it on the ground. I grab a bottle of champagne from a cooler in my truck, pop the cork. As we drink the lights of the city are below, hazy streetlamps cutting through the darkness. Maybe it's nothing to brag about, maybe most people don't give a shit about electricity unless it's gone, but my family's responsible for almost everything that happens down there, from lighting the houses, to opening the garage doors, to heating up everyone's split pea soup. Everybody is always fawning over the police and fire departments, calling them real American heroes, letting them be in parades, buying their charity beefcake calendars. Would they be anything without having the electricity to make their alarms ring, though? Would they be so great if their dispatch radios were dead and they weren't receiving any of the pertinent details of fires and robberies and murders? Every night I rescue everyone from total darkness and no one has ever asked me to ride on a float.

I pour champagne into our flutes and clink glasses and take a gulp. Then my cell phone rings. It's my dad.

"Let it go to voice mail," Flor says.

"It might be an emergency," I say.

It's not really an emergency. A crow has crawled into the house through the heating vents and perched itself on the top of Antonio's bookshelf. This is old hat for Flor and I, something that happens at least once a month, something we've grown accustomed to, but which is freaking out my dad.

"Hang tight," I tell him. "We'll be home in few minutes."

The next day, I'm eating a burrito in the cafeteria when I see Hollenbeck riding away from the graveyard on a moped. He's got a duffle bag slung over his shoulder and his vestments are flapping behind him in the wind. I run down to the parking lot to give chase, but before I get to my truck I hear the crackle of Vincent's radio telling me I should get out to Chet's grave quick.

When I get there, Vincent and Uncle Jimmy are standing over the grave looking into Chet's empty casket.

"I don't know how Hollenbeck got past me," Vincent says. "He must've cut a hole in the fence or something."

I race over to the rectory. Hollenbeck's sitting on his porch drinking some ice tea. He's paging through his newspaper like nothing's happened, like everything's normal. I bound up the stairs and lift him up by his shirt.

"Where the fuck are my brother's bones?" I yell.

Hollenback laughs at me then, long and hard, a hardy, mocking chuckle, full of garlic from his lunch, and Jesus Christ, something ratchets up inside me and I can't stop myself, I pull out my taser and blast that fucker, blast him really good this time, crank up the voltage full throttle and hold down the trigger until his cackling stops and that shit-eating grin slides from his jackass mouth and the tears falling down his cheeks combine with his drool sliding over his lips into one long sad gushy river that slides off his chin and onto the floorboards of the porch.

Luckily for Hollenbeck, Ethel comes outside and slaps the taser out of my hand.

"What is wrong with you?" she yells. "He's a helpless old man."

Ethel pushes me away and then she gathers up Hollenbeck. All of the color from Hollenbeck's skin has disappeared, his body looks spectral, so pale, like he might glow in the dark.

When I get back home, Antonio's sitting on the front steps. At first it looks like he's playing with a large stick, but when I get closer I see that it's a femur. Antonio's crows are sitting near him in the grass, watching me.

"Where did you get that?" I snap.

"From there," he points.

I find Chet's bones in a duffel bag on the front porch. I grab the bag and run out the door. I want to rebury Chet quietly, before Flor sees him again, before any of her old feelings for him are dredged up again. On the way to my car, I try to yank the femur from Antonio's hands, but he's got it pulled tight to his chest, won't it let go.

"No, Uncle Bryce," he says. "This is mine."

"I'll get you a different bone," I tell him. "A leg bone from a bear. Or one from a cougar. But I need this one back now, okay?"

Antonio shakes his head no, no, no. I don't have time to bargain with him, to explain how much this might scar him in later life, so I just wrestle his father's femur away from him. I'm expecting a shitload of tears and howling, but Antonio doesn't react at all. He looks through me, like he's in a trance.

"You're going to die in a car crash," he says. "Your truck is going to flip over ten times, but that isn't going to kill you. Your truck will explode after the crash and you'll suffocate in the fire, trapped inside."

And Jesus Christ, again, it's just like a reflex, my anger, like a cresting wave that can't be stopped from flipping itself down onto a sandy shore. Before I can stop myself, I yank my taser from its holster and quickly zap Antonio in the arm because not right now with the death shit, okay? It's hardly even a tase really, just a little pop, something that might jumble your brain for a second, make your arms go limp so you let go of your father's leg bone. I let go of the trigger before he even pees his pants, okay? Yes, yes, after I do this I know I've done something truly messed up, that I've overstepped my bounds as both a parent and uncle, maybe overstepped my bounds as a human being, that I've done something awful.

Antonio is howling now. I think about bribing him with a new bike to quiet him down, but I don't even get to offer the bribe because Flor sprints downstairs to see what's wrong. She's wrapped in a towel, her hair still wet from the shower. I'm holding my taser and Antonio has two fresh burn marks on his arm and it doesn't take a whole lot for her to add everything up.

"I'm sorry," I tell her. "He did his soothsayer thing to me and I overreacted."

I kneel down in front of Antonio to give him an apology hug, but before I can wrap my arms around him Flor scoops him up and carries him inside. I don't get to explain anything about the bones, about Hollenbeck.

"Go!" Flor screams before she slams the door. "Leave now!"

For a while, I stand outside our house yelling apologies to the two of them from our driveway. I tell them about how I'll change. I tell Flor that I'll do whatever she wants me to do to make this right. I tell her how much I love her and Antonio and how I can't live without them. I yell out apologies for a long time, but Flor doesn't unlock the door. I decide to give her some space and so I leave to go bury Chet. Before I go I set the femur on the welcome mat as a peace offering to Antonio. Then I grab the duffel bag with the rest of Chet's bones and drive to the graveyard.

After I dump Chet's bones back into the casket, I shut the lid and use the plow on my truck to push the dirt back over his grave. The bottle of champagne is still in the cooler in my trunk and even though it's flat, I finish it off while I watch the old men fishing on the banks of the river, their bait slapping down into the water whenever they throw out a cast.

When I get back home that night, Flor and Antonio are gone. No note, no nothing. I call Flor twenty times, over and over, but she never answers. I flop down on the couch and try to figure out where she and Antonio might have gone. Are they with one of my relatives? At a hotel? As I'm sitting there mulling everything over, the power goes out. It is really weird and eerie when the rattling of the world goes suddenly quiet, when the whirring and white noise that is constantly all around you flips off. I look outside and everything is dark. I pour myself some whiskey and I sit on the couch. After a while I remember there's a flashlight in one of the drawers in the kitchen. I dig through the drawers. I desperately pat them down. I keep thinking the flashlight is in one of them. I keep thinking the flashlight will be the next thing I touch. I flail my hands around, searching, but I don't ever find the damn thing.

WINNIPEG

I'm on the wrong side of history and I've got a vodka-soaked sea sponge shoved up my ass to help me forget. Reichmann's got one up his shithole too, but Schliess can drink regular and so he's sipping directly from the bottle of hooch and then passing it to us to douse our sponges some more. We're hiding in a church rectory outside Winnipeg, all three of us ducking into a large armoire full of vestments whenever we hear the Americans outside.

We know each other from the military hospital in Saskatoon. My tongue was cut off by an American sergeant who liked to collect tongues; Reichmann's lips and jaw were blown off at the Battle of Thunder Bay. Schliess can't talk because there's something wrong with the way his mouth connects to his brain. The doctors wired my jaw shut and wrapped Reichmann's head in bandages, leaving only a slit for his eyes. After we all got well enough to sit up, the doctors pushed our beds together and tossed us an old sign language book to share. Then the doctors laughed. We laughed along with them or did whatever each one of us did in lieu of laughing: snorting (me), or stomping our foot on the ground (Reichmann), or laughing regular with a lot of drool (Schliess). We laughed because the Americans had just occupied Montreal and it was only a matter of time before everything that was still considered Canadian collapsed or exploded. We laughed because even though it was only early April, it was already 106 degrees. We laughed because why in the hell would we learn something new when we could just pass our vintage porn mags back and forth to each other and point at some woman's snatch and give a universally understood thumbs-up or thumbs-down.

A few days after the doctors gave us the sign language book, the Americans shelled our hospital and killed everyone but a few people in our non-talking wing. The three of us hid in the rubble until Reichmann pulled out his sketch pad and drew a picture of a pretty woman with large breasts. He wrote the words "This is my wife!" underneath the picture. Then he wrote the words "She's in Winnipeg!" Then he underlined both the words and the tits for emphasis. Schliess took the picture and circled her tits and wrote "Does she have any sisters?" and then there was much porkchopping and substitute laughter between Schliess and myself but then Reichmann wrote "I want to see her before I die!" underneath the tits and then there was a long and uncomfortable silence between all three of us that was luckily broken up by an American bomber flying over and dropping some more bombs and us ducking under some convenient pieces of rubble.

We all knew getting to Winnipeg was a suicide mission, but what the fuck wasn't? We loaded up our backpacks and started to trudge. All three of us were still in our early thirties, just old enough to remember how the seasons used to change, cursed with enough years on this tumbleweedy Earth to remember deciduous trees and spring breezes filled with scents of cut grass and lavender. When we stopped to rest on that first night, I got into an argument with Reichmann about how our lives would've been much better if they weren't yoked to these idyllic memories of snowflakes melting on our tongues or of us jumping into piles of raked leaves. I told him we'd be much better off not knowing anything other than blistering heat and constantly pitted out T-shirts.

"If we'd grown up in this perpetual sauna," I wrote to him in the dirt with a stick, "the heat would feel just fine to us."

Reichmann grabbed the stick from me, scribbled his response.

"Humans can get used to anything, no matter how deplorable or sad. We just reset our expectations and find happiness in our revised baseline."

"And that's a good thing?" I scratched back.

Even though his face was heavily bandaged I could see Reichmann roll his eyes at me. And when I handed him back the writing stick to respond he snapped it in half over his knee. Face or no face, Reichmann was being a dick and I started to look for a new writing stick to tell him that fact.

"Forget about him," Schliess motioned to me. "For once let's just have a nice, quiet dinner."

In his previous life Schliess worked at a shelter helping teenagers whose lives had gone awry. While the war had hardened him, there was a part of him it hadn't touched, something soft in the way he moved his hands that could always calm me down.

"Fine," I nodded.

For dinner, I smashed up a banana I'd picked from a roadside tree and poked it through the gap between my teeth with the wrong end of a plastic spoon. Reichmann crushed up a mango with his mortar and pestle and once everything was minced into a fruity sluice he used a straw to suck the slurry through that hole in his cheek he was currently calling his mouth. Schliess tore at a piece of beef jerky and then dabbed away all the blood from his gums with his sleeve. The sun wasn't going down anytime soon, but when I finished eating I tied a rag over my eyes and laid down on the partially melted yoga mat that I'd recently found in a ditch.

Sleep came difficult for me now. Before the war I'd been a chemist, working on cholesterol meds at a pharmaceutical company. When the war started, I immediately volunteered my services to a lab inventing chemical weapons. Like everyone else in Canada, I was caught up in the fervor of defending our borders from the southern invaders who wanted our remaining water and cooler air. While I absolutely understood the potential applications of my work while I mixed compounds and ran my beta tests, it's a different thing altogether when you see a chemical weapon you've invented, one I'd named Black Krezcent, get dropped on a regiment of Americans bedding down near Calgary. I watched on the video screen as the drone's door opened and the metal canisters tumbled through the sky and cracked open in a field and a mist of odorless microparticles spread through the air and hit the Americans' skin and then their mouths quickly opened in screams and their skin peeled away like husks and their bodies began to flop on the ground like pieces of bacon in hot grease. Yes, I drank the celebratory champagne just like everyone else in the lab, I screamed "Hooray!" and "Liberty!" with the correct gusto, slapped fives with my coworkers until my palms were nearly blistered, but when I closed my eyes that night and for every night since, those dying flopping fucking skinless American soldiers are the only thing I ever see.

The three of us were caught by an American patrolman on the fourth day of our trudge. He looked about sixteen. He'd just shot a toucan and he was filleting it when we came through the brush.

The kid got the jump on us, grabbing his machine gun before we got to our knives. I thought we were done for, that we were headed to a prison camp or he'd gut shoot us and leave us to bake in the noonday sun, but then Reichmann got down on his knees and begged for mercy.

"Mercy?" the American asked. "Seriously?"

Reichmann gave him a number of exaggerated nods to convince the kid that he should grant us clemency, but the nods were punctuated by a bunch of gritty gauze flopping around on Reichmann's face, which made everything less convincing.

"If you would've got the jump on me would you be so kind?" the American said. "The fuck you would."

Even though he knew it was a lost cause, Reichmann kept begging. He handed the American the picture he'd drawn of his wife and the kid looked at the drawing and said, "Wow, does she have any sisters?" and Reichmann groaned and shook his head glumly and some ropey blood slid off what used to be his chin and onto the ground and the kid laughed at that, laughed at Reichmann's missing face and his bad luck and the bad luck of the three of us. Fortunately, while the boy was distracted with his giggling, Schleiss yanked his throwing knife from his ankle sheath and chucked it into the kid's throat and then Reichmann jumped on top of the kid and stabbed him over and over in the eyes and the chest. When he was dead, we sat around his fire and ate the remainder of his toucan and smoked the rest of his cigarettes.

We trudged on. All the lakes and rivers and marshes had dried up years ago and the ground was newly gouged from tanks and bitten by army boots. There was no such thing as dignity anymore so sometimes we stripped naked and found shade in one of the thicker dead oaks. If the biting flies weren't horrible we rested, Reichmann pulling out his journal and using a charcoal pencil to render one of many massacres he'd witnessed over the last two years. Reichmann had been an abstract painter before the war, but now he only drew realistic black and whites. He never saved any of his drawings. Whenever he finished one he'd just tear it up or light it on fire.

"Why don't you keep them?" I wrote to him once. "Someone needs to document the atrocities we've seen, don't they?"

Reichmann paused for a second, but then he wrote back, "At least none of us has kids," which was not exactly what I asked him but which was an appropriate response and something extremely fortunate.

When our sponges dry up, Reichmann and I pull down our pants and soak them again. Who knows where Schliess heard about it, but when he saw those sea sponges in that abandoned food coop his eyes lit up.

"Way better than regular tampons!" he wrote. "No possibility of toxic shock!"

While I'm bent over resoaking my sponge, a priest walks into the rectory. He's holding a baseball bat but he drops it onto the marble floor when he sees I've got a machine gun pointed at his chest.

"What in the fuck, guys?" the priest says. "This is still God's house."

The priest is harmless and I lower the gun. Schleiss points the priest toward the bottle of vodka on the counter and he takes a long swallow. As the liquor passes over his tongue, I see him wince. Then he grabs his jowls and moans.

"Bad tooth?" I point.

"Killing me," he says. "Can't chew, can't drink."

"Hold on," I motion and I go into my backpack and give him one of my extra drinking sponges.

"Soak it in vodka and shove it up your ass," Reichmann explains.

The priest is reluctant, but we all spread our cheeks and show him we're not fucking with him and finally he shrugs his shoulders and pulls down his black pants and shoves his sponge in there too.

We keep chugging. And like usual I get sad. I find a piece of paper and a pencil and I scribble a question to the priest.

"What if I've done unspeakable things?" I write. "Can I ever be forgiven?"

There've been dozens of Black Krezcent strikes since that first one. I can't help but think if I hadn't mixed those chemicals together I might be free of this crushing guilt. Schliess has written me long notes in the dirt trying to absolve me from blame, telling me that if I hadn't invented it, someone else would have probably invented something worse. While I appreciate his attempts to cheer me up, no amount of Schliess's dirt scribbling can get those images out of my head.

The priest isn't answering my question, he's staring out at a gutted-out train station across the street so I tap him on the shoulder. I hold the piece of paper with my question on it right in front of his face. You need to have a huge amount of faith to still wear the collar, especially in this heat, and when you start drinking it probably slips away just like for everyone else. Schliess and Reichmann shake their heads at me, so tired of how maudlin and sentimental I get when I'm blotto.

"For fuck's sake," Reichmann writes. "Leave the man alone so he can absorb the liquor through the blood vessels in his sphincter just like the rest of us."

We wait until nightfall to go find Reichmann's wife. The priest guides us through the sewer tunnels so we can avoid the American patrols. The heat underground is incredible and the rats down there look like loaves of waterlogged bread. We stumble over each other in the dim light until the priest tells us we're here and then we all climb up a ladder and slide a manhole cover out of the way. Now that he's standing in front of his house, I can see the fear in Reichmann's eyes. He's not sure he wants to go through with this.

"Maybe it's best if she thinks I'm dead?" he motions to us. "Or maybe she's already moved on? Or maybe she won't believe it's really me?"

While we're waiting for Reichmann's courage to kick in, Schleiss walks over and pounds on the door. Soon a woman yells out to us.

"We've got no more bread," she says. "And no more vodka. And we all have raging cases of gonorrhea. Best to be on your way."

Reichmann walks over and pushes the note he's written through the mail slot. In a minute the door swings open and Reichmann's wife is standing in front of us. She keeps looking up at Reichmann's bandaged face and then back down at the note. She's shaking her head like it can't be true, but then Reichmann holds out his hand and she studies it, takes her fingers and runs it over the lines crisscrossing his palm. And then she throws her arms around Reichmann's neck and sobs. The priest is bawling now too, as most normal people would be, but Schliess starts to giggle and I join him, snorting like I do, because while this reunion is certainly poignant, Reichmann really pulled one over on us—his wife is flat-chested as fuck.

We're all hustled inside. Sitting at the dining room table are two other women. Schleiss and I find out that Reichmann's wife actually does have sisters, nice friendly ones. The dark-haired one is named Elyse and the blonde one is Cara.

Slowly the night turns into a party, not like the drunken keggers we used to have when we were young, but a decent party just the same. At some point Cara pulls a guitar out from the crawl space and all of us climb up to the rooftop terrace. While we stand there there's a quick northerly breeze full of fresh flowery goodness that fills our nostrils for just a second and Cara starts to strum her guitar and we do whatever it is we do in lieu of singing, we hum or we lightly moan or we slap our knees or we just close our eyes, shut the hell up, and listen.

OUR MOM-AND-POP OPIUM DEN

Our mom-and-pop opium den is being forced out of business by a big-box opium den. Our regulars are pissed. My father and I are despondent. I stare across the street at the "Grand Opening" banner spread across Opium Depot's facade, at the huge inflatable gorilla tethered to their roof, at their strolling mariachis, at their free hot dogs and free pony rides. I wonder if we'll be out of business in weeks or just days.

"Fuck Opium Depot," Jake Stensman tells me. "Screw those corporate fucks."

Jake's twenty-three years old, a Marine just back from Afghanistan. He's wearing a gray T-shirt with the words "Semper Fi Mofo" silkscreened on the front of it. The tattooed names of his dead friends scroll down his tanned arms like a royal proclamation. Last week he told me he hears his dead friends screaming whenever he closes his eyes. His dead friends scream and scream and they don't ever stop.

"Live local! Buy local!" he yells across the street.

Jake's red-faced now, but soon he'll be so high that all the ruddiness and anger in his body will float away. In a few minutes, he'll be lying in one of our smoking beds and the only thing he'll care about is taking an occasional breath.

"How about a protest?" Allen Cho suggests. "How about we walk around in a circle in front of their entrance wearing sandwich boards and chanting?"

Allen Cho's daughter drowned in a lake two years ago. Allen sees his daughter in his dreams, her long, reedy arms reaching out to pull him down into the murky deep. There's always lots of mud on her face and algae and sticks intertwined into her billowing hair. Other than some bloating, Allen says, her face looks exactly the same as the day she died.

"If it didn't look like her," he jokes, "I wouldn't need to be here, right?"

While everyone looks across the street, I sit down at my desk to decide which bills to pay this month. Electric or water? Gas or phone? I wonder if our power got turned off would anyone notice? Could I light some scented candles from my dead mother's curio cabinet and just tell everyone I'm trying for more ambiance?

I rip up a past due notice about our mortgage and my father pads around stuffing everyone's pipes. The doctors tell me to surround him with familiar things, to keep him on a regular schedule. The doctors tell me he will have good and bad days. At first, they tell me, the bad days will be equally bad for both him and me. Then the bad days will get subtly better for him and significantly worse for me. At some point my father's realization of what a bad day is or isn't will slide from his consciousness and this fact will cleave my heart into a number of tiny pieces but luckily leave him unfazed. He'll get a lot better when he gets a little worse, the doctors say.

"How about a huge sale?" Jennie Frontiere asks. "Show their asses you're here for the long haul."

None of our asses is here for the long haul, especially Jennie's. She's got bone cancer and opium is the only thing that deadens the ache in her arms and legs. Sometimes she tries to knit mittens for her grandchildren, but after a hit on the pipe her knitting needles slide out of her fingers and clatter to the floor.

"What about promotional punch cards?" Jake suggests. "Ten pipes, the eleventh is free?"

The line snaking out Opium Depot's door curls down our block. I scan it for familiar faces, for any customers of ours they've already poached. My dad keeps busy. He fluffs pillows, brews a fresh pot of decaf.

Our place looks almost exactly the same as when he opened the doors thirty years ago. Red and gold walls. Silk tassels hanging from every goddamn thing. I've worked the register since I was eight and for the last twenty years I've watched hundreds of people kill themselves slowly and convincingly. It makes me sad to think I probably won't get to see our current group of regulars meet their maker too.

My father pushes dirty sheets into the washing machine, pulls clean ones from the dryer. Outside our doors, all bets are off, but inside here, he's still a huge help to me. Inside here, he can sometimes make me forget he forgets.

"We've outlasted everyone before," he says. "We'll just do it again, right?"

The memory loss chatrooms tell me to pick my battles, to try to keep his stress level low. All the commenters advise me to conserve my energy for the long haul ahead. Why deliver bad news when you'll need to deliver the same bad news in five minutes, they say, and then again two minutes after that?

"Of course we will," I say. "We'll bring those assholes to their knees."

Allen, Jake, and Jennie shuffle back to their beds, jonesing for their next hit. I walk around and light their pipes. When I'm done I flop down on an open bed and my father lights me up.

"Maybe this will clarify things," I yell out to everyone before I inhale. "Maybe we'll get some better ideas after this."

So yes, instead of fighting Opium Depot, what we decide to do in this case is to wait it out, hope for strength or illumination to descend from above. What we do in this case is smoke.

In this case?

In every case.

When I wake up later there's a bright yellow piece of paper stuffed into my mouth. It's a promotional flyer from Opium Depot. All my regulars have them in their mouths too. Someone from Opium Depot waltzed through our doors while we were zonked out and leafleted our asses.

My father's asleep on his cot. He used to be a light sleeper, awakened by the tiniest floorboard creak. Now you have to poke him in the chest for a minute straight before he'll open his eyes.

"Help me gather up those flyers before everyone wakes up," I tell him. "If they find out how cheap it is over there, we're finished."

My father rubs the sleep from his eyes, threads his toes into his flip-flops. I grab his forearm, steady him as he stands. His knees are bad from all the up and down that occurs in this business. He had his right knee replaced last year. His left one is giving him trouble now, clicking and popping. I wonder if we should just skip replacing it. Maybe he'll just forget he's in pain? Or maybe soon he'll forget what pain even is? I jot down a note to ask the doctors about this at our next appointment.

While we grab the flyers, I look over at the counter and see that while I was nodding off my dad bought a huge bag of fortune cookies at the Asian market down the street, snapped the cookies in half, and then pulled out all the fortunes. There are at least a hundred fortunes spitballed on the counter. This is the second time my father's done this in the last week, leaving crumbs all over the countertop and the floor. Lately he treats fortune cookies like they're pull tabs or scratch-offs, like one of them will be a winner, like he's searching for a phrase he's waited his entire life to be told.

"Dad," I say. "We talked about you leaving here alone, right?"

"I went out for a little bit," he says. "I needed a break. I needed some goddamn sunshine."

After our visit to the doctor last week, my father and I had a frank discussion about his condition, about the safety measures we needed to implement to keep him safe. The doctors keep suggesting I put him in assisted care, with prepared meals and around-the-clock care. Strangely, the doctors always clam up whenever I ask them where to get the money to pay for all that.

"I don't like the new rules either," I tell him, "but we need to keep you alive."

My dad opens and closes his hands while we talk, balling his fingers into fists and then fanning them out wide. The doctors warned me there might be some initial frustration when the new rules were put in place, that things between the two of us might get physical. My guard is up. My dad's in good shape, he still looks like he could land a decent uppercut.

"Are you forbidding me to come and go?" he asks.

Today's a good day for him, a day of complete sentences. Today's not a day of him hiding underneath our kitchen table or pissing in the snake plant. Today's not a day of him calling me William, his dead brother's name. Today my father isn't cupping his forehead and telling me how his brain feels swollen, that it feels like there's a gallon of water sloshing around inside his skull.

While we talk, I stare across the street at Opium Depot, at that huge inflatable gorilla perched on their roof, its hands held above its head in victory. Their parking lot is packed, cars circling around waiting for a spot to open up. Their valets sprint past our window in their blue windbreakers and black pants, tracking down cars they've stashed in their overflow lot.

"It's for your own good," I tell my dad.

My dad stares me down in the same way he stared me down when I was in high school and I smashed his Buick through our garage door. I look down at the floor to avoid his gaze. While I'm looking down there I see a black ant skitter across the air vent toward a fortune cookie crumb, but before the ant gets there the air conditioning kicks on and it gets shot up in the air. The ant floats there above the ground for a second, defying gravity, its tiny legs moving willy-nilly until he falls down into the vent and probably dies.

"I can," my dad says, before losing his train of thought.

"I still am," he says, his voice quiet, drifting off.

Was everything always this dire? No, no, not this dire. Two years ago, I returned home from grad school with big ideas. I hired a graphic designer to print glossy brochures. I installed Wi-Fi. I bought a new couch for the lobby. I repainted the bathrooms sea-foam green, stocked healthy snacks in the vending machines. I marketed our space as a perfect option for a bachelor or bachelorette party. My father was skeptical about the impact these improvements would have on our bottom line, but he stopped questioning me after our quarterly profits shot up 14 percent.

Unfortunately around this time, my fiancée, Susie, broke off our engagement. We'd already sent out save-the-date cards and booked the reception hall. We had the cake tasting, I'd rented my tux. Then one night, after a company happy hour, she fucked her boss, Rodney Pargo, in my car.

"You were practical," she told me, "but I won't be happy with practical. I need some excitement. I need someone who gets my nipples hard, someone like Rodney, who drives around with a ladder in the back of his Chevy Tahoe in case he wants to break into the zoo and make the tigers or bears watch him make love."

I'd already planned out my life with Susie, was shocked at her sudden betrayal. I turned to the pipe to stop thinking about how much I missed her round ass and her raunchy sense of humor, how much I missed that great lasagna she made. I turned to the pipe to forget how my car smelled like cherry lube whenever I turned on the heater. I turned to the pipe because no matter how much fucking Windex I sprayed Rodney Pargo's greasy footprints would not come off my windshield.

This morning I call the memory loss helpline and tell them I'm scared of my father wandering off.

"Tape a black carpet square in front of your door," the counselor on the phone advises. "He'll think it's a hole. He'll think it's the abyss and he won't want to fall inside. It works great."

"That sounds cruel," I say.

"A lot of people say that," the guy says, "but you need to realize that at this point in your father's life safety and cruelty sometimes walk hand in hand."

I duct tape the carpet square to the floor, watch as my dad bends down to peer into its inky void.

"How did that get here?" he asks. He's leaning away from the carpet square like it has a gravitational pull, like he's going to be sucked in.

"It's a floor mat," I tell him.

"I hate that I can't see the bottom of it," he says. "I hate that I can't see where it ends, you know?"

Our regulars are in between pipes. Jake sets down his tattoo magazine and walks over to stand next to me. Last week he brought in a six-pack and we sat in the alley and had a heart-to-heart. He told me how his father died at Costco lugging a shitload of Greek yogurt to his truck, how my dad reminds me of his dad.

"You need a break?" he asks. "I can watch the shop if you wanna get out of here for an hour."

I look over at my dad. He's sitting at the counter now, picking at a roast beef sandwich, studying the carpet square from across the room. Soon his upper body starts to do this rocking thing, back and forth, over and over. I put my hand on his shoulder so he stops. "That would be great," I tell Jake.

Everything still reminds me of Susie and Opium Depot is no different. It's tastefully lit, just like her condo was. There's a greeter at the front door whose dark hair is sort of close to the color of Susie's dark hair. The greeter is wearing a blue polo that looks kind of similar to a blue polo I remember Susie maybe wearing once or twice.

"I'm Samantha," she says. "Would you like a bed?"

I scan the floor. I've got to hand it to them, they've got this all figured out. Rows and rows of beds with individual separation screens. Identically dressed pipe tenders walking around in T-shirts and khakis. A central dispensary behind bulletproof glass. Security cameras mounted to the ceiling every twenty feet. The air conditioning is cranking like we're in a casino.

I remind myself that I'm not here to enjoy myself, I'm here to spy. As I lie down Samantha gives me a choice of recently released movies to watch on the flat-screen TV mounted to my bed.

"Or," she tells me, "I can queue up something from our extensive music library."

Before I walked in here I conned myself into thinking that the service wouldn't be as personal, that they'd treat their customers like cattle, but Samantha gives me a scalp rub and asks me how my day is going and she actually seems genuine about it.

Maybe the product will be watered down, I think. Maybe that'll be the thing we can hang our hat on. But then Samantha lights my pipe and I inhale and the smoke fills my lungs and every piece of sadness and stress I hold between my shoulder blades floats away and all the chatter in between the hemispheres of my brain finally shuts the hell up. My jaw unclenches and a thin stream of drool slides out of my mouth and falls to the newly carpeted floor. A delicious fatigue comes over my body and suddenly I don't give one shit about competing with Opium Depot, I just want this feeling forever.

"Where have you been?" Jennie Frontiere asks when I walk in the door later that evening. "Jake called and called."

Every day Jennie Frontiere brings a can of soup for lunch, heats it up in the microwave. Two months ago, she organized a potluck. While no one else brought anything and I was the only one who ate the macaroni hot dish Jennie brought, my father and I certainly appreciate her efforts at making our place feel a little bit more like home.

"There was a fire," Allan says. "Not 911 worthy, but pretty decent size."

I run into the office, see that the left side of the desk is charred. My dad is standing there running his fingers over the burnt wood. Jake's standing next to him. Sometimes I see a switch light up in his brain, some old synapse grab hold, and he'll snap at me in a way he would have snapped at me twenty years ago, and even though he's yelling at me for being a dumbass, it's just wonderful to see my old judgmental father alive and in fine form once again.

"He walked in here to grab a pen and then a minute later the smoke alarm went off," Jake says. "I should've stuck closer to him."

My dad is eyeing the desk cautiously now, like it's going to suddenly catch fire again, like the wood has disappointed him in some way by being flammable, like the desk can't be trusted to be a desk anymore. Lately whenever his words leave him, he grabs items he knows he should remember—alarm clock, table lamp, pen—and holds them out to me, desperately shaking them in my face until I reveal their name.

"Let's just go lie down," I say, putting my hand on my dad's shoulder.

My dad slaps my hand away. I can tell he's wondering who I am, who gave me the right to touch him. At first, his eyes are filled with confusion and outrage, but then they shift to scared.

"It's me," I say, holding out my palms to show him I mean no harm.

He stands there for a minute, looking me up and down.

"Just you," he says. "Okay."

I pull his arm over my shoulder and we walk over to his cot, his bad knee clicking like a metronome with each step.

Later that night, after my dad is in bed, I light up and dream about Susie. I dream about when we went on that riverboat architecture tour in Chicago. It was one hundred degrees that day and I remember my shins sweating and the sweat pooling up in my tennis shoes and the smooshing sound my shoes made when I walked back up the gangplank.

I wake up to two burly men in tracksuits standing over my bed. One grabs me under my armpits and one grabs my ankles and they lug me out the door.

"Hello?" I yell out. "Help?"

Everyone else is zonked out. The men carry me out into the parking lot and shove me into the backseat of a Lincoln Town Car.

"Are you gonna kill me?" I ask them. "Because you should know that I am already doing a good job of doing that myself."

The men don't answer me. We drive downtown and pull up in front of a building with a sign "The Uplands Group, LLC" on the side. The men yank me out of the car and shove me up some loading dock stairs. They push me into an office and I see Steve Windom sitting across the desk from me.

I recognize Windom from the covers of all the opium trade journals. He's clean-shaven, wearing a navy-blue suit. There's a neutral paint color in his office, low-pile carpet, no shitty tassels anywhere. His autobiography *How to Kill the Dragon* was required reading in one of my business classes in grad school and so I know a lot about him—how his father used to beat him with an electrical cord, how he dropped out of high school at age fourteen, how he ended up on the street turning tricks to pay for his habit. I know how he found Jesus and got clean and how he started cleaning toilets in a den and clawed and scratched his way up the corporate ladder to ruthlessly conquer the opium business. While I'm excited to be in the same room as him, I know from the chapter on negotiation in his book that I should not show any excitement at all.

"I apologize we had to bring you over here like that," he says. "But I always like to discuss business face-to-face."

Windom doesn't waste time with chitchat. He reaches into a drawer and pulls out a brick of opium and slides it across his desk. The brick looks like black clay. It has red veins snaking up inside it like little rivers.

"You've had an incredible run with your shithole, but that's over now," he tells me. "This is your going-away present. And after you take it you're immediately going to go back and shutter your place up forever."

I look at the brick and my mouth begins to water. I force myself to stop staring at the brick, at its luscious color. I stop thinking about how wonderfully bitter it probably tastes. Instead of looking at the brick, I stare at the wall behind Windom. There are a bunch of photos of him hung there, one of him windsurfing on bright blue water and another of him snowboarding on chalk-white snow. While I look at these pictures of Windom I wonder why he's arrived where he has and I have not. Maybe it's because I've always had trouble telling the difference between luck and fate, maybe because they've always seemed like the same thing to me. I wonder if there is something more than hard work and smarts that makes a difference? How come some people always have the wind at their back and others don't? How come some people are programmed to see every setback as a challenge and others see it as proof they're doomed?

"My shithole's worth more than one brick," I tell Windom, even though it probably isn't. "There's so much history there."

Windom takes out another brick out and slides it across the desk.

"Here's to history," he says.

There's enough dope here to keep me high for a year or to kill me really good in a month. There's enough dope here to say fuck all to my regulars and my dad, to quit worrying about them altogether, to hole up in a hotel room with a prostitute who will let me pay to call her Susie even though her real name is Marilyn or Monica.

I pick up the bricks, one in each hand, feel their heft. I think about how I don't owe anything to anyone, about how I never promised anyone a place of refuge, about how my dad would forget about my betrayal in two minutes.

While I mull over this decision, I notice a picture of Windom's wife in a frame on his desk and goddamn it if she doesn't look like a dead ringer for Susie. I start to think about how much I loved Susie and how I thought we were going to be together forever. Instead of betraying my father and our regulars, I call bullshit. Bullshit that Windom gets all of this and I get nothing. Bullshit that he wants to crush my family business and bullshit that I'd make it any easier for him. Even though my hands are shaking like hell, I push the bricks back across Windom's desk. I see a glint of surprise cross his face, but it's quickly replaced by anger.

"Bad call," he says.

When I get back to the den, Jennie and Allen are playing cribbage. Jake is standing over the top of them, looking at them as they clack their pegs around the board. My dad is asleep on the counter, his cheeks flushed. It's windy outside and I watch as two Opium Depot employees climb up on the roof to batten down their inflatable gorilla.

Soon I light everyone up. It's hard not to think that each time I do this it will be my last, that soon the cops will show up and slap an eviction notice on our door. In the last few days, I've started to slow down my movements, savoring every second we have left here. Each time I light up one of our regulars, I say a quick good-bye to them under my breath.

I sit down in a recliner and close my eyes and drift off. I wake up to the sound of breaking glass. While I was sleeping someone chucked a large rock through our front window. The rock is sitting on the black floor mat. I walk over to get a closer look. Windom has written the words "Only the beginning!" on the rock and signed his name.

"Dad?" I call out.

There are a ton of fortune cookies broken open on the counter.

Most of them are spitballed, except one that's been flattened out that reads: "Higher ground is higher ground."

While I'm standing there, I hear sirens. I look out the window and see fire trucks, ambulances, police cars surrounding Opium Depot. There's a crowd gathered in their parking lot. People keep pointing to the roof. What they are pointing at is my dad, dressed in his pajamas, his legs dangling down near the neon "U" in Opium Depot's sign. I race across the street, fight my way through the crowd.

"I'm his son," I explain to one of the police officers. "Let me go up there and talk him down."

The cops lead me to a service ladder mounted to the side of the building and I climb up, walk slowly across the roof toward my father.

"It took you long enough," he calls out. He pats down a spot next to him and I sit, dangle my feet over the edge, just like he's doing.

"The air up here reminds me of the lake cabin," he says. "It's crisp."

I know exactly what he's talking about, he's totally right, the air up here has a little bite to it, smells lightly of lavender when the wind freshens, just like the lake cabin we used to rent when I was young.

"And there we are over there," he says, pointing to our building.

I see all chipped paint on the south wall, notice all the beer cans and potato chip bags on our roof. I look down at all the people standing in the parking lot below us, their hands on their hips, waiting for something bad to happen. The security guards on the roof are inching closer to us, talking into their walkie-talkies.

"Maybe we should go down now?" I ask.

"One more minute," he says.

He closes his eyes and takes in a lungful of air. I do the same. While I've got my eyes closed my father stands up and runs. At first I think he's going to jump off the side of the building, but then I see he's running toward the gorilla. I watch as he pulls a knife from his pocket and stabs the gorilla in the calf. Next he takes his knife and shivs the gorilla in the foot. There's a massive rush of air past my face, a wind that drives me back. The gorilla's arms fall to its side then its hips start to shimmy. It happens so quickly, the air trapped inside there that's now free. The gorilla's head bows toward my father and he slices open its forehead then jabs the knife into the gorilla's chest as it folds. The security guards are running at him now, a bunch of them, all of them screaming at my father to stop. It's too late. The last of the gorilla's air slides out of its body and its black skin floats down and covers up my dad. At first he stands tall, but soon he melts under its weight, kneels down, disappears into its darkness.

ACKNOWLEDGEMENTS

First off, thank you to Kate and Theo for their unflinching love of a person with a serious burrito addiction. Next up, to all the Jodzios, Diethelms, Condons, McDermotts, for years of showing up to every damn reading I've ever done even if they had to drive through apocalyptic winds and thigh-high snow. To the wonderful Emily Condon, who is owed way too many favors to count. Gracias to Eric Vrooman, whose charitable early readings brought many of these stories back from the abyss. A lengthy hat tip to the octopus queens of *Paper Darts*, Meghan Murphy and Jamie Millard, for always using their eight arms for the greater good. To the early readers of these stories: Lara Avery, Dennis Cass, Tony D'Aloia, Marcus Anthony Downs, Thorwald Esbensen, Luke Finsaas, Alex Helmke, Baker Lawley, Ross Nervig, Maggie Ryan Sandford, and Robert Voedisch; thanks for the late-night gin and wisdom about words. Thank you to Adam Johnro and Neil Vacchatani for twenty years of inside jokes. Thank you to my editor, Dan Smetanka, whose judicious eye made these stories shitloads better than they started. Thanks to my agent, Ethan Bassoff, whose skill in talking me down from ledges, both high and low, is unparalleled. To all the incredible people at Soft Skull and Counterpoint, especially Megan Fishmann, Sharon Wu, and Kelly Winton, for their enthusiasm and diligence in getting this book out into the world. A final thank you to the Minnesota State Arts Board, the Sustainable Arts Foundation, the Loft Literary Center, the Jerome Foundation, and Pen Parentis—I am humbled and grateful for your financial support and your confidence in me.

PUBLICATIONS

"Knockout," *Mixer*; "The Indoor Baby," *Indiana Review*; "The Wedding Party," *Tampa Review*; "Inside Work," *The Tangential*; "Lily and Annabelle," *Austin Review*; "Ackerman Is Selling His Sex Chair for Ten Bucks," *MnArtists*; "Alliances," *Paper Darts*; "Someday All of This Will Probably Be Yours," *Twin Cities Noir*; "The Piss Test Place," *Whiskey River*; "Great Alcoholic-Owned Bed and Breakfasts of the Eastern Seaboard," *Brooklyn, Vol 1.*; "Cannonball," *Matrix Magazine*, winner of the Lit Pop Award; "Winnipeg," *The Atlas Review*; "Our Mom-and-Pop Opium Den," *Normal School*, winner of the Normal School Prize; "Athens, Athens," *Salt Hill*; "Duplex," *The Adirondack Review*, winner of the Fulton Prize.